Ashes and Steel

For those who burned, and those who still rise.

For my son and daughter,
and everyone who listened, believed, and helped me keep
writing.
For those who didn't thank you for showing me who I truly
am.

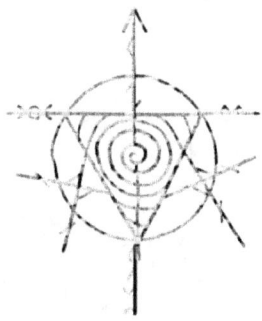

THE REALM

HALEWYCK

Dreadsmere

SKAL...

aerthwyn

The Rift

Vaelorya

Lorensburg

Direfel

NORTH

3
era

Author's Note

When I started writing *Ashes and Steel,* I didn't set out to tell a story about witches or fae.

Honestly this book is near and dear to my heart because of the emotional tole it has taken to write it. The concept came from witches but then it just kept spiraling into new ideas. Ashes and Steel is my baby and I'll never forget it.

— Kayla Johnson

COMING SOON

Rift and Ruin
Even memory burns when the Rift calls your name.
The story continues as time fractures, hearts are tested, and the tether between witch and fae faces its breaking point.

Ashes and Steel is the first book of the Ashes and Steel series

Kayla Johnson

TRIGGER WARNINGS & DISCLAIMER

This story contains themes of trauma, grief, emotional distress, coercion, and recovery.
It also includes violence, manipulation, psychological control, and loss.
While these elements are woven through the fantasy setting, they mirror real human pain and healing.
Please take care of yourself as you read.
All characters, events, and settings in this work are entirely fictional.
No real names, people, or events were used or referenced.
Any resemblance to actual persons, living or dead, is purely coincidental.

The Ashes and Steel Saga explores cycles of faith, ruin, and rebirth.
It is not meant to glorify harm, but to reflect how light survives even in its aftermath.

CHAPTER 1
Ash on the Wind
Joanna

It rained this morning, but it didn't matter. Ash
sticks.

You can scrub until your skin burns, change your
clothes, even burn the rest, but it lingers.
In the seams of your hands.

In the back of your throat.
Behind your teeth, like something unsaid.

 It clings to you the way grief does. It's stubborn and impossible to shake.

The square always smells of smoke, even when it doesn't.

I walk fast, hood up, head down. I know the rhythm by now. The grime from last week's burning is still wedged in the cobblestones. No one cleans them. No one talks about them. The stones hold memory better than people do.

Halewyck doesn't bury its dead; it waits for rain.

The marketplace leans crooked around the square; stalls jammed together like gossipers. The baker's voice is always the loudest corner, shouting over his ovens, flour drifting like smoke. His laugh makes you sick; too loud, too proud, cutting through the market like a cleaver. He

pinches girls more often than dough, and no one calls him out loud enough to matter.

The church looms above everything, its bell tower shadow reaching across the pyre like a hand that never moves. You can hear the bells even when they don't ring. Always waiting. Always warning.

The pyre waits in the center. Always the center. They don't tear it down between burnings. They leave it standing, char-black against pale stone, wood stained with what won't wash away. You can smell it before you see it.

Her name was Nina. Sixteen. Quick wit, quicker tongue. One of the few girls who didn't lower her eyes when a man barked. I liked her for that, though I'd never have said it aloud.

She told off the baker in front of half the village told him maybe if he spent less time pinching girls and more time watching his flour, his bread wouldn't burn.

That was it. That was the moment. Three days later, they dragged her to the square. Said her dough rose too fast. Said her eyes held something unnatural. Said her mother whispered too much.

They say a lot of things right before the fire starts. Mercy is just the word they use before sharpening the knife.

I didn't really know Nina, but I knew her type. And I liked her type. Until the moment they burn, and then everyone pretends they never spoke her name.

But I remember her wink across the market when she caught me nearly laughing at her sharp tongue. I remember the way she walked through the square like it belonged to her, chin high, eyes bright.

Ash covers memory as neatly as it covers stone.

Mama used to say omens don't scream they settle in the quiet.

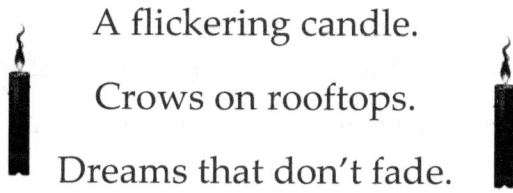

A flickering candle.

Crows on rooftops.

Dreams that don't fade.

They burned Mama, too. Years before Nina. Different lies, same kindling.

Papa wasn't much better, a drunken bastard who thought fists were as good as words. Tess took care of him. Old Tess never said how, just came home one night with blood on her hem and told me to pack a bag. I didn't ask questions.

We don't live in Mama's cottage anymore; I can't sleep in the place where she was dragged out screaming. Better Tess's crooked, herb-stinking house than ruins filled with ghosts.

I don't talk about any of it. Not out loud. Not even to myself.

But the air feels different today. Heavy. Waiting. Salt on the breeze, smoke in the chimneys. Two ways the world can choke you; pick one.

The fire won't catch properly. I crouch low, coaxing it like a nervous animal until the flame finally takes. The herbs go next, rosemary, sage, mint. Do I need them? No. But pretending I do helps. Routine is its own kind of magic if you let it be.

Tess would say the same, in her gravelly voice that never softens. She'd also say I'm wasting good mint. She'd swat my hand, scowl, then go right back to muttering over her own bundle as if every word she spoke was law. Her curses sound like blessings if you don't listen too close.

There's a bundle by the fire, still tied. Tess gave it to me like it was a riddle.
"You'll know," she said. I hate when she says that.

But tonight, I do.

There's a pull low in my spine, something shifting, something sharp. I light three candles: protection, truth, and the third I don't name. Then I untie the bundle with more hesitation than I want to admit.

Inside:

a black candle

A handful of crushed petals; carved stones etched with symbols I've never studied but that feel like bruises in my palm; and a folded note.

Mama's handwriting. My breath stops like I've been punched.

When it begins,

light the black candle.

Speak nothing but truth.

Let no man name you.

She always had a flair for the dramatic.

Still, I light it. The flame burns blue. Of course it does.

"My name is Joanna," I whisper. "Daughter of the woman they burned. I've hidden. I've lied. I've bitten my tongue until I bled. But I'm done pretending I'm nothing."

If that makes me villain, fine. Villains survive longer than saints.

The room tilts. The shadows crawl. My ears ring with silence too loud to bear. Then the floor vanishes.

This isn't a dream. Not the usual kind. It's too clear, too sharp. My breath fogs. The ground is smooth stone, cold beneath my palms. The air tastes like honey and ash.

This is Dreadsmere.

Halewyck whispers of it as a serious, mystical realm reduced to shadows. A place where dreams breathe and every shadow leans close to listen. Power hums here, where mist holds shape instead of fading. Stone arches curve too smooth; halls stretch and fold like both ruin and cathedral. It feels wrong and so very right all at once more real than the waking world.

And she's here.

Not a shadow. Not blurred or distant. Real. Or close enough.

She stands beneath a pale archway, arms crossed, watching me like she's already read the ending. Her hair is dark and wild, her eyes sharp, her expression unimpressed with everything including me.

"You took your time," she says.

"Sorry," I answer, dry. "Didn't realize I was supposed to follow your schedule."

Her mouth twitches. Not quite a smile. She steps closer. Not threatening, just curious.

"Who are you?" I ask.

She shrugs. "Wouldn't you like to know? Let's just say… your favorite mistake."

Then, like she's answering a question I didn't ask:

"We ruled together once. And gods, we were good at it."

Images strike too fast to hold: a crown, a throne, war, a kiss, her hand over mine, a map drawn in stars, power that tasted of salt and blood.

My knees give out, but she catches my wrist before I fall. Her grip is steady. Real.

"You and me," she says. "Empresses. Soul-bound. Tell me that doesn't sound hot."

The world fractures.

"What's your name?" I ask.

"Morgan."

It fits too well.

The dream tears like paper in water. "Look for the crow," she says. "You'll know." Then she's gone.

I wake on the floor, cold, still wrapped in the aftertaste of burn. The candle is gone. So is the bundle. But the room still smells scorched. Like truth. Like her.

Morgan.

I whisper the name just to feel it. It fits too easily. Outside, the wind rattles the shutters like it's asking to be let in. Something has changed, and for the first time in years, I'm not sure I want to keep hiding.

On the wood floor lies a single black feather. I pick it up.

"She's real," I mutter. "Of course she is. Why wouldn't I find a crow feather in my house to prove it? Or maybe I just want a badass empress with a crown. Who wouldn't?"

My boots crunch frost as I step outside, heart hammering. The woods lean close, black branches netting the pale sky. I don't think. I just move. Fast. Like my body got the memo before my brain did: hot dream girl; this way.

It's exactly the kind of thing white girls do in scary movies run into the woods chasing whispers, candles still burning at home, ignoring every omen. The kind of choice people shake their heads at after the credits roll.

And I am absolutely doing it.

Branches snap underfoot. Cold air bites my throat. My palms are sweating, feather clutched tight.

I don't know what I expect to find. Honestly? Probably nothing. But also? Possibly the crown-wearing fever-dream of a woman who showed up in my sleep, handed me emotional whiplash, and called me soul-bound.

So. You know. Tuesdays.

But the village isn't far. A door slams. A shutter creaks. A voice rises, too loud for the hour.

I glance back. Faces appear. The butcher boy with his knife. Melany at her window, smile too wide. Tess on her stoop, muttering curses into the dawn.

They see me with the feather. They see the direction I'm walking. That's all it ever takes.

Not proof. Not fire. Just a moment. A shadow. A hush, like the breath before a spark.

The pyre waits in the square. The church shadow stretches long. The bells don't ring, but I hear them anyway.

"Witch."

Not shouted. Not chanted. Just a single word, soft and sure.

And I know: it's already too late to hide.

CHAPTER 2
The Hunt
Morgan

Caerthwyn never sleeps.

Even when the moons sink low and the wind dies; something still hums beneath the soil like the heartbeat of a god that refuses to die. The air is warm and thick, sweet enough to choke on. It smells of rain that never falls and flowers that never rot. You could almost forget its poison when it tastes like honey and milk.

Bioluminescent moss crawls over black stone, threads of blue fire pulsing slow as breath. Trees older than memory twist upward, bark rippling with faint veins of light. Their roots glow underground, binding everything like bones under skin. The flowers never wilt here. They glow too bright, too perfect, too alive. Their colors sting your eyes if you look too long—petals like spilled blood, dew that glitters like gold dust.

The sky shifts in ways that shouldn't be possible. Violets bleed into gold, green fades to silver, and sometimes the horizon breathes. The stars move like they're alive. Once, I thought they were souls. Now I know better.

Even the ground glimmers with each step, sparks rising like fireflies. The rivers mirror the skies so completely you forget which way is up. You could drown standing still.

People call it paradise.

I call it a cage.

The Courts like to say the factions exist to keep balance. Balance, order, tradition words they use like spells to keep everyone quiet. But it's not balanced. It's control. Divide enough people, and they'll never realize the bars are gilded.

If you're told who you are from the moment you can stand: Hollow, Antlered, Gilded, Dreadmarked, you stop wondering what else you could be. You wear the mask long enough and forget the shape of your own face. They call it identity. I call it chains polished bright enough to blind you.

I've seen the factions break people down until they forget how to breathe without permission. The masks, the horns, the jewels, the marks they're not symbols of pride. Their shackles dressed up as power.

Caerthwyn glows because it feeds on obedience.

The Factions

The Hollow Court

Secrets dressed as prophecy. They move like smoke; robes stitched with paper charms that flutter as they walk. Their masks are bone or mirrored glass, reflecting back every fear you've ever had. Their voices are soft, slow, too calm. Every word sounds like an ending. When a Hollow looks at you, it feels like they've already written your death. You just haven't read the page yet.

The Antlered

Fury dressed as faith. They wear horn and iron like crowns, some grown from their skulls, others nailed on until the blood stains their temples. They smell of sweat and pine and old war. Their laughter is thunder; their silence is warning. When they march, the ground moves with them. Stand beside them and you'll feel the weight of their conviction. Stand against them, and you'll never stand again.

The Gilded

Cruelty dressed as beauty. Their armor gleams so bright you'd think they swallowed the sun. Their smiles are knives dipped in honey. Perfume masks the rot, and no one dares mention the stench of old blood beneath the roses. They toast you with jeweled cups and slit your throat before your drink cools. The Gilded are the Court's favorite illusion that rot can sparkle if you polish it enough.

The Dreadmarked

Survival dressed as silence. Ink crawls their skin,
alive, shifting if you stare too long. Every mark
whispers its own curse. Their veins look like
shadows trying to escape. They move quietly, like
they've learned not to disturb their own ghosts.
Their eyes burn—steady, unflinching—and when
they meet yours, it feels like judgment. Everyone
looks away. No one ever forgets being seen.

And then there's me.
Factionless. Feral, as they like to call it.

I wasn't born into the Court. I was chosen.
Pulled in. Collared, with their laws and told them
to sit pretty. I didn't. I laughed. Bit back. Broke
their rules just to hear them crack.
They call me wild because I refuse to kneel.
Because I remember what it felt like before the
leash. Because I don't wear their colors or bow to

their symbols. And when they call me *pet,* I make sure they remember I bite.

That's Caerthwyn's truth.

Not peace. Not unity.

Just cages painted in different colors, arranged so neatly, they almost look like harmony.

And above all, the oldest law: witches and fae must never touch, never want, never bind.

They tell us it's because of the story—the one every child knows. Once, a fae and a witch tied their magic together, and the knot tore the world apart. A Court vanished. Rivers turned to ash. The skies broke open. Balance shattered.

So, we learn the words before we can read them.
Fear them. Hunt them. Burn them if you must.

Which is funny, considering the face that haunts my dreams belongs to a witch.

The hall of decrees is marble and menace.
Everything gleams too bright. Light cuts at angles
meant to blind. Torches hiss with blue flame,

smoke curling in thin ribbons like breath from a
dying god. The factions gather in their rings of
gold, bone, blood, shadow each pretending to
listen, each waiting for the chance to strike.
The Elder stands at the center. His robes weigh
more than his mercy. His voice slices the silence in
half.

"The witches multiply," he says. "Their kind
threatens our balance. This hunt must be swift.
Absolute."

I raise my hand.

"Question. Are we sure you're not just calling
everyone who annoys you a witch?"

The sound that follows is all sharp breaths and the
clatter of pearls hitting marble. Lena shifts beside
me, calm as ever, adjusting her bowstring like

she's already calculating the distance between us and the gallows.

"Try not to get executed before they send us out," she murmurs. "Dragging your corpse back would be terribly inconvenient."

"Nice to see you care."

"I don't."

The Elder's eyes find me; black, cold, too still.

"Morgan. You will lead this hunt."

Of course I will. I bow, lazy enough to earn another gasp.

"Didn't realize I was your favorite disappointment."

The Hollows whisper behind their masks. The Gilded smile like they smell blood.

In the Antlered row, Zane stands taller than the rest. Antlers strapped to his helm, black hair falling like oil. He doesn't smile. Doesn't blink. Just watches me the way predators study patterns before they strike.

"You will take Lena," the Elder adds. "She will keep you… focused."

"Oh good," I say. "Send the one person who cares."

"Tragic," Lena mutters.

The silence that follows could crush lungs. The Elder flicks his hand, and the air breaks with the sound of dismissal.
We turn our backs on the gold-lit hall and step into the dark.

The forest begins where the light ends. The moment we cross the threshold, Caerthwyn's glow sticks to my skin like ash. The air shifts thicker, older, breathing in its own rhythm.

The dirt path hums faintly beneath our boots. Sigils are burned into the ground thin gold veins threaded shallow under the soil. They say protection spells. Alarms, I say. One wrong step and the whole forest will sing our location.

Lena nudges one with her boot until it sparks. "Charming, breadcrumbs, but lethal."

I grin. "Don't worry. I'll protect you."

She scoffs. "Gods, no. You're the one who needs saving."

The forest swallows our voices whole. Fog drifts between the trees, silver and slow, catching light in ways that make the air shimmer. The trunks pulse faintly like veins under skin. Somewhere far off, something cries soft, long, not human.

I keep my eyes forward. I don't think of her. I don't think of dark hair and clever eyes and a voice that sounds like the moment before a storm.

I don't think about how her name feels when I say it.

Joanna.

Lena doesn't press. She knows better.
We walk until night folds over us.

The fire crackles low, painting everything in amber and smoke. Lena sharpens her arrows; I lie on my back, watching the canopy breathe. The stars here shift faster than they should. They blink like eyes. I wonder which ones are watching.

Sleep comes slow, then all at once.
"zzz… huh… whuh… mmm… Jo…"

Lena dry as sand:
"Did you just snore, wake yourself up, ask what, and then moan a girl's name?"

My eyes snap open. "What?"

"Exactly like that. Except the last part was *Jo*. Clear as day."

Heat crawls up my face. "You're making that up."

"Wish I was, funny thing, though we're supposed to be hunting witches, and you're half-feral in your sleep for *mmm... Jo.*"

I sit up, smirking.

 "Half-feral? That was full feral. I commit. Want me to prove it?"

"Please," she says without looking up.

"You wouldn't survive saying my name like that awake."

For a moment, I actually shut up. Her mouth twitches. Almost a smile.

"Dreams make you braver than you are. Out here, you're just loud." She says.

The fire dies slowly. The night breathes heavily. Eventually, I sleep again.
Joanna didn't come this time. Memory does. A Gilded room. A velvet voice in my ear: You'll

always be mine. Nails scrape me raw, and pleasure and pain knot together until I can't tell which I'm supposed to want. My body betrays me like it always has.

Chapter 3

The Lesson
Morgan

They called it a chamber, but it felt like a stage. A perfect circle. Candlelight dripping gold over polished stone. Shadows folding inward as though the room itself were leaning close to listen. The air was thick, humming with old magic, neither warm nor cold, but alive. It moved against my skin like breath.

I didn't need to test the walls to know I wasn't leaving.

The doors opened with a long, low **creeeak**. Cold air crawled in. The scent of incense tangled with iron and wet stone, sharp enough to sting. The guards didn't shove me. They didn't have to. My boots did the work for them, scraping across the stone too loud, too human. The sound echoed up into the tiers, swallowed by the dark.

The audience was already waiting.

Dozens of them. Rows stacked high, faces lost to shadow. Their eyes were what caught the light finding them and staying there. Hungry eyes. Measuring eyes.

My breath faltered. The chamber itself seemed to breathe around me, steady where I wasn't.
Then, Lena.

Gods. My best friend.

She stood near the far wall, rigid as stone. Her face was pale, her jaw set in defiance. Our eyes caught like magnets snapping together. She mouthed a single word: *No.*

Her lips trembled around it.

I wanted to look away but couldn't. I wanted to tell her I was fine, that this was just another test, that I'd Walk out of here. But even lies seemed dangerous now.

The crowd stirred.

"She's pale already."
"Another one to break."

Their laughter cracked through the air like whips. Heat crawled up my neck. I forced my chin higher.
Then silence.
Sharp. Immediate. Like the breath before a blade falls.
She entered.
Ines.

Storm-gray robes edged in gold. Hair coiled into a crown so tight it gleamed in the light. She didn't walk; she arrived. The sound changed when she stepped inside, like the air shifted to accommodate her.

The chamber bowed in its own quiet way. Even the torches leaned.

Relief hit me in a single, poisonous rush. My shoulders loosened. My lungs remembered how to work. Because I'd been waiting for her...half dreading, half needing the sight.

Ines didn't need to speak to claim the room. She was gravity in human form. The silence that followed her wasn't fear. It was awe.
She stopped across from me, her presence precise as a blade's edge. Her eyes were lightless silver calm, assessing, impossible to hold for long.

"Sit," she said.

She didn't raise her voice. She didn't have to.

The command slid through me clean and absolute. I sat. My body obeyed before my mind had time to

protest. A chair scraped softly against the floor behind me as if it had been waiting.
The sound rang out too loud in the hush.

"Lesson one."

The Elders murmured their approval from above. I refused to look at them.

The air thickened, just slightly. Not enough to suffocate, but enough to feel it settle across my chest like invisible hands. I straightened my spine against it, breath sharp and deliberate. The pressure wasn't cruel. It was precise. Measured.

And then it was gone.

The relief that followed was dizzying. My lungs expanded too fast; the air burned cold in my throat. I almost gasped.
Her voice broke the silence, soft and even.

"Control requires awareness. The body must listen before it resists."

Her tone was not unkind.

She took a single step closer. The light shifted with her, catching the fine edges of gold that traced her sleeves. Everything about her was symmetry and stillness, crafted like ritual.

The Court leaned forward. The air hummed. Even magic seemed to wait for her next breath.

"Lesson two."

Her gaze swept me like a current. It wasn't invasive, but it felt like being read like every thought I'd ever had was being held up to the light and studied for shape.
I tried to hold her stare. Failed. It wasn't fear exactly. More like gravity again pulling me toward her even as I tried to stay upright.
Lena dropped her eyes to the floor. Her hands were fists at her sides.

Ines's expression didn't change. If anything, it softened.

"Discipline is not punishment," she said. "It is refinement. To resist without understanding is to waste strength."

Her words carried no malice. Only fact. Only calm authority.

The air around her shimmered faintly, heatless, colorless, like the world itself was bending to make room for her will.

I realized my hands were trembling and pressed them flat against my knees.
Her gaze flicked down. Noticing. Not judging.

"Lesson three."
Her voice was soft, clear enough to carry to every corner.

"She is not broken," she said. "She is learning."

The Elders nodded, their robes whispering as they shifted. I didn't look up. My pulse drummed in my ears, matching the rhythm of her words.

Then Ines moved closer so close I could feel the warmth of her presence, the soft current of air stirred by her breath.
She didn't touch me. She didn't need to.

"Breathe," she murmured.

And I did. Automatically.

The word moved through me like command and comfort at once.

Her eyes met mine again, steady and unflinching. There was no cruelty in them, only clarity. She wanted me to understand something. Something larger than the lesson itself.

"This is restraint," she said, voice just for me. "Power without chaos. Mercy that does not weaken. To stop is sometimes harder than to strike."

The words sank deep, threading through my thoughts before I could stop them.

She stepped back, the spell breaking with distance. I felt it immediately the ache of space between us. My lungs caught on the absence of her focus, like stepping into cold air after standing too near a flame.

Around her, the chamber blurred again. Candles flickered. The crowd's attention wavered, restless now that the heart of the moment was over.

Only Lena stayed sharp in my vision. She looked furious. Heartbroken. I didn't blame her. When she turned and walked out, I wanted to call her name. I didn't. The word would've cracked in my throat.

The doors closed behind her with a slow, final thud.

The chamber exhaled. Voices returned, low and murmuring. Cloaks rustled. The audience began to move again, their hunger sated for now. Ines remained still.

She looked at me, head tilted slightly, studying. Not like prey. Like potential.
"You understand now," she said softly.
I nodded, because it felt right to. Because at that moment, I did.

Her mouth curved almost like approval.

"Discipline," she said, "makes devotion possible."

Then she turned, her robes whispering across the floor. Each movement was deliberate, ritualistic, closing the space she'd opened between us.

The doors opened for her without touch.
When they shut, the sound was absolute.
For a long moment, I sat there, alone in the echo of her voice.

The air smelled faintly of gold and smoke.
My hands were steady now. My chest is still tight,
but not from fear. From something I didn't want to
name.

Ines had done nothing to me, not really.
But she'd left something behind anyway
a silence that felt like her hand still hovering near
my heart.
And me
I'm left trembling.

Awake.

I am ashamed to admit it.
And gods help me, craving the next lesson.

Kayla Johnson

CHAPTER 4
Village Whispers
Joanna

The forest was supposed to quiet me.
It didn't.

By morning, half of Halewyck had apparently
seen me crawl out of it like some stray cat learning
to walk upright. The stories spread faster than
sparks in a dry field because in this town, rumor is
the only thing that ever catches fire.

The butcher's wife swore I was carrying a dead
crow under my arm. The seamstress claimed I was
naked and chanting. Old Marla, who can't see five

feet past her stoop, told anyone who'd listen that I flew.

Impressive, really, considering I can't climb a fence without bruising both knees.

The truth is simpler: I couldn't sleep. I walked. That's it. People walk. I just happen to do it at the worst hour, into the worst patch of trees, with a feather in my pocket and someone else's name rattling through my ribs. Perfectly normal behavior for someone not trying to get burned alive.

The morning light bleeds gray and blue, thin like smoke. My hands are already stiff from cold. Every window I pass looks like an eye, every shutter half-open like a lid caught mid-blink. On the way to the well, I rehearse excuses like lines in a play no one's ever going to believe:

"Checking the snares." Except I don't own any.

"Needed firewood." At midnight? Sure.

"Clearing my head." Of what? My mother's ghost?

"Sleepwalking." My favorite. If anyone presses, I'll tell them to take it up with my unconscious body.

It doesn't matter. Once Halewyck decides you're a witch, you could spend the whole night knitting socks for orphans, and they'd still swear you were hexing the yarn.

By the time I reach the square, the air smells of yeast and coal smoke. Baker's shouting, vendors clattering, the usual noise only thinner when I pass.

The well waits in the center like a throat. The bucket ropes creak as I pull. The sound echoes too loud in the hush that follows me everywhere now. A boy points.

His mother yanks his hand back like he's touched hot iron. But not before he whispers it. Witch.

Nina would've smirked at that. She would've crouched to his level, told him he was right, maybe taught him a better curse word to shout louder next time. That's what I liked about her she sparked. And maybe that's why she burned.

Halewyck doesn't forgive sparks. It stomps them out before they can catch.

Now they're looking at me like I'm her second act.

Melany is at the well, of course. Her braid is perfect. Her dress spotless. Her smile practiced in mirrors. She's flanked by girls who wear ribbons like armor.

When she sees me, she tilts her head just so.

"Rough night?" she asks, voice dripping syrup.

"Sleepwalking," I say flatly.

Her friends giggle. She doesn't. She just watches me, eyes bright with the kind of kindness that cuts.

And for a dangerous second, I wonder what it would feel like if she looked at me softer. Kinder. I shove the thought down hard enough to bruise. The stable boy is at the next pail. He doesn't laugh. Doesn't speak for me either. His silence lands harder than her smirk.

By the time I leave the square, my excuses feel brittle.

Tess finds me outside her shop. She presses a bundle into my hands without a word. Sage. Rosemary. Bark streaked with dark veins like ink frozen mid-flow. The smell is sharp, green, almost medicinal.

"You need to stop making it easy," she says.

"I was walking."

"Not at that hour. Not in that direction."

"I couldn't sleep."

Tess lifts one eyebrow like I've just tried to lie to the woman who raised me. "Then stay awake in your own bed. People are watching. They watched your mother, too."

That one lands.

Tess doesn't apologize. She never does. Maybe she's right not to. She killed once to keep me safe, and I still wonder if she'd do it again.
Before I can answer, a crow drops onto the roof above us. Its claws scrape the wood. It tilts its head, beak gleaming, eyes sharp as flint. Another joins it. Then another. Three in total.

"Count them," Tess mutters.

"One for sorrow," I recite automatically. "Two for joy. Three for a girl stupid enough to let herself be seen?"

"Four," Tess corrects, though there are only three.

"Always four."

She disappears back into the shop before I can ask what that's supposed to mean.

I tuck the herbs into my cloak and keep walking. The crow follows me to the edge of the square, then veers off with a rough cry like laughter. Behind me, voices start stitching again.

"She's her mother's daughter."

And softer still, nearly lost under the clatter of wagon wheels:

"We should've burned both."

I don't turn. I don't need to. The word has already found me, curling through Halewyck like smoke.

Witch.

Not a scream. Not yet. But once it's spoken, it clings harder than ash.

By the time I'm past the last house, the sun is climbing pale and weak. The fields smell of damp earth and the promise of rot. My boots are heavy with mud; my fingers ache from gripping the pail too long.

The forest waits ahead quiet, watchful. The same one I left hours ago.

I should go home. Instead, I step back into it. Mist hangs between the trees like breath. The ground gives under my feet, soft and cold. My cloak drags through ferns still wet with dew. Somewhere far off, a stream hums under the noise of birds waking.

It should be peaceful. It isn't.

Something about the silence feels arranged, like the woods are holding still on purpose.

I find the clearing without meaning to the one with the hollow log I used to hide trinkets in. I kneel

beside it. The bark is slick. Inside, nothing but dirt
and a single feather, black as pitch.

I don't remember leaving it there.
The air shifts behind me.

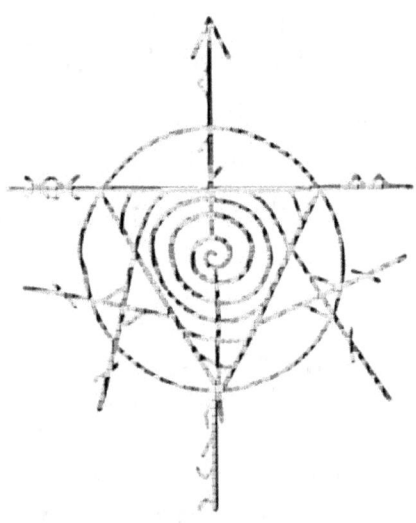

Chapter 5
Reflections in Flame
Morgan

Sleep finally drags me down like chains after endless memories. When I surface, it's always the same place. The lake, black as glass. The light glints off the lake's surface; fractured, metallic, unnatural. The sky was bruised purple, heavy with stars sharp enough to cut. The air tastes like metal and honey, thick as breath before a scream.

And she's here: The witch.

She's already there at the water's edge like she's been waiting. Arms crossed, brows raised, voice flat as a blade.

"You again?"

I grin. "Yeah? Come here often?"
Her lips twitch. "Only when I feel like chasing after some dream girl I can't seem to get away from."

"Oh, so you do like me?"

"In your dreams."

I blink at her slowly, deliberately. "You do realize… we are in a dream, right?"

That earns me a smile. Quick. Unwilling. Real. It hits like a spark in a dark room.

She shakes her head. "What are you even doing here? Haunting my dreams again?"

"Call it haunting if you want," I shoot back. "But you wouldn't keep coming back if you hated it."

Her voice dips sharper. "Not really. Feels like I keep getting trapped in here by you."

"Then I guess you're stuck with me. Try not to look too disappointed."

That gets me a look sharp enough to gut me. She doesn't back down.

She exhales like it costs her.

"I just can't shake the feeling that I know you. And that this is real."

The tether hums under my ribs, restless and raw. I smother it with words.

"Yeah. Me too. I've been looking for you."

She frowns. "Dreams don't usually leave bruises."

I grin, wicked. "Kinky. What have we been doing in here, exactly?"

Her cheeks flared. "What the hell? Not that kind of dream."

"Oh?" I tilt my head, feigning disappointment. "So, you don't want that?"

She sputters, flustered. "Excuse me?"

"Hey," I shrug. "You're the one chasing me."

Her jaw tightens. "Gods, you're infuriating."

"I try."

And then the tether snaps taut.

Pain lances through me, white-hot, splitting me from the inside out. I stagger, clutching my ribs.

She folds the same second I do, her hand pressed to the same place as if we are mirrors.

The lake ripples. For half a heartbeat I swear I see a crown floating there black, jagged, heavy as stone before the water swallows it whole. Above us, the stars twist into lines, constellations knitting themselves into a map I almost recognize. Then they collapse inward, gone.

A crow cries overhead. Sharp. Out of place. The sound splinters the air like a crack in glass.

Our eyes lock through the agony. Mirrors again.

"You...You felt that?" she chokes, breath ragged.

"Yes." The word tears out of me, gritted and feral. "Try not to look so damn satisfied while it's killing me."

She huffs a laugh that cuts like glass. "Satisfied? You look pathetic."

"Maybe," I rasp, ribs screaming. "But you can't look away."

The lake shatters. The sky caves in. Her face is the last thing left before the dark swallows everything. The dream drops away, but my body doesn't follow.

The air is thicker now. It's still electric and wrong. The smell of the lake clings to me. It smells like iron, rain, and honey. I can taste it when I try to swallow.

My eyelids flutter but won't open. My chest feels pinned, ribs caught under invisible weight. My breath comes shallow and thin, as if something is sitting on it.

I can't move.

Not my hands. Not my mouth. Not even my tongue.
Somewhere near the foot of the bed, something shifts.
A whisper.
A step.
Soft. Bare.
Then another.

The air moves around it, bending slightly, like it's making room.

I try to twitch a finger. Nothing. The effort feels like screaming underwater.

Another step.

I can see through slits of vision, colors blurred at the edges. The corners of the room glow faint blue, as though moonlight has soaked through the walls.

A figure moves through it. She's Tall. Wrapped in shadow and silk that gleams faintly with motion. Her hair trails behind her like smoke. Her feet touch the ground, but they don't sound like feet.

The closer she gets, the thicker the air becomes. It hums with static, and my heartbeat stumbles trying to match it.

I can't move. I can't speak. My lungs rattle like glass in a box.

She stops beside the bed.

She leans forward slightly. She's beautiful. Her face is hidden, half-shadowed, but the gleam where her eyes should be is sharp and knowing.

She lifts her hand. Slowly. The air crackles with each inch of the motion. The air between us hums. My skin heats beneath it, even though she hasn't touched me.

The sound grows louder deeper than thunder, closer than breath.

Her head tilts, curious.

The faintest hint of a smile curves her lips. Small. Certain.

My throat works uselessly. My body convulses once, shallow, enough to draw a ragged breath.

Then she leans closer.

Ashes and Steel

Her voice slides through the dark, so quiet I almost
think I imagined it.

"Wake soon."

My body stays locked, trembling. My breath
returns in small, fractured gulps.

For a long moment, the only sound is the rasp of
air between my teeth.

And beneath it, faint but unmistakable
the tether, still alive.

I know she's gone. But the imprint of her presence
lingers, cold as shadow, heavy as touch.

She wasn't part of the dream.
She came after.
She was here.

Watching.

Waiting.

CHAPTER 6
Threads in the Dark
Kael

The woods were never silent. Not to me. Every branch hummed, every root whispered, every shadow bent toward the same hidden loom. Threads strung across the dark; silver and pale, some drawn tight, some frayed, some trembling like they'd snap if I breathed too loud. Most people can't see them.

Most people are safer that way.

But I was born hearing the weave sing. The Courts keep me close because of it. Close, and leashed.

They want my sight, not the truth that comes with it.

Tonight, the threads pulled east through the trees toward a cabin that shouldn't have stood here. Small, crooked, stubborn, its beams carried more weight than stone should. It breathed like it had lungs.

Two strands glowed brighter than the rest, older than vows, hungrier than any Court chain. One burned hot and reckless, the other pulled slow, unyielding, steady as bone. They wrapped and wound and tightened the whole forest around them. The woods themselves leaned forward, waiting for the knot to close.

A crow landed above me, oil-dark feathers gleaming like a wet blade. Its bead-black eyes fixed on mine.

"Yes," I told it quietly. "One burns too bright. The other pulls too hard. And if they knot everything else will snap."

The crow croaked once and vanished into the dark, a sound like a hinge closing.

The threads thrummed on, alive and restless. I could feel the cabin holding its breath.

Zane

The Courts put us on watch duty again.

Kael stood beside me, still as a post but twitching at the edges, fingers brushing the air like he was plucking at strings only he could hear. I didn't ask. I'd heard enough of his visions to know when the world itself was listening.

The cabin crouched ahead, a glow in its single window. Crooked walls, a door that leaned like it resented being upright. Ordinary to anyone else. But not to Kael. And not to me, either, if I'm honest.

The woods pressed in. The smell of damp earth and frost bit at my lungs. Somewhere overhead a crow shifted, its claws scratching bark. The air felt ready to split.

The first figure appeared, a tall shape cloaked against the cold, wings folding tight as she stepped toward the door. A Fae. Morgan. I know Morgan.

We trained together once.

The next figure followed, smaller, sharper, her presence bending shadows around her. A witch. Kael inhaled sharply. "If they meet," he murmured, "the weave will knot."

I kept my eyes on the cabin. "Then we don't interfere," I said. "We watch. We remember. Because if the world tears open, we'll need to say where it began."

The Fae was already inside. The witch lingered at the door. The whole forest leaned forward, waiting.

The threads thrummed louder. Binding. Hungry. And I knew whatever tied itself in that cabin would drag the rest of us with it.

CHAPTER 7
The Pull
Morgan

I wake choking.

The dream clings like smoke, heavy in my lungs. My chest burns like I've already lost someone I can't remember, and waking didn't fix it. The fire's dead. Ash cold. Air damp.

Lena's voice slices through the dark, calm as ever.

"So. Who's Jo?"

I bare my teeth in something pretending to be a grin.

"Wouldn't you like to know? Jealous already? Careful, Lena you'll catch feelings."

Her face doesn't shift. Her voice stays flat as stone.

"You wish. Whoever Jo is, she won't be half as good as me. But you said her name again. Louder this time. You moaned really loud in your sleep, Morgan."

Heat floods my face. "No, I didn't. I don't moan; I narrate. With flair. With impeccable timing. I'm the one who makes other people moan for me."

She doesn't blink. Deadpan: "Sure. You just scream people's names for fun. You did it three times, louder each time like you were finishing."

My brain short-circuits. "She's not…I'm not…I didn't; stop. Just stop."

But the world tilts anyway. Not pain, not fear, something worse. A hollow pull deep under my ribs, like a rope tightening around my lungs. My chest cramps. My hands claw at my sternum before I realize I'm even moving. Each breath leans me forward, like gravity finally picked a direction.

Lena stands fast with her sword in hand, eyes narrowing. "Morgan. What the hell are you doing?"

I press my palm against my chest and laugh, sharp and breathless. "Losing my mind, apparently."

"You look like it."

"It's not nothing, Lena. I feel… pulled. Like something's out there waiting for me."

"You don't even know what it is."

"No," I admit, grin crooked, too wide, "but it feels like I should go anyway."

Her nostrils flare, but her voice stays steady, practical. "Well, I'm not following you into that forest fire straight to a pyre. Or worse, branded an enemy of the Court."

I huffed out a laugh. "They've already branded me. What more can they do?"

Something flickers in her eyes, gone before I can name it. She doesn't follow. She doesn't try to stop me.

The pull throbs again. I stand and turn toward the trees.

"Fine. Walk into ruin if you want," Lena says at last, voice flat as a wall. "But don't ask me to follow."

I don't wait to give a response. I just leave.

The forest swallows me whole. Branches snag my clothes, whispering as they slide away. Fog clings to my face, damp fingers smearing across my skin. Flowers shimmer in the dim light. They blink like eyes watching. They'd be pretty if it wasn't so creepy.

I try to stop and breathe, but the second I do the cramp in my chest clutches harder, claws digging in. So, my choice is to move or suffocate. Dream girl and heart palpitations. Great," I mutter.

The joke dies quickly. It's too quiet. Even the insects aren't impressed.

The fog thickens, heavy as smoke. Shapes swim in it until a single standing building appears angled roofline, crooked walls, a door leaning on rusted hinges.

A cabin.

Small. Weathered. The kind of place that remembers things.

The pull inside my chest eases the second I step close, like the ache was just waiting for me to get here. My knees are weak. My body stills as if to recognize the structure before me. Like I've been here before, but I haven't.

A crow calls once. Sharp. Close.

I don't know what's inside.

I go in anyway.

Joanna

I wake with tears streaking my face. They aren't quiet tears. They're ugly, raw, and loud. My chest heaves like someone scooped it hollow, the same wound that opened the day they burned my mother. I wipe my cheeks, but it doesn't stop. My hands shake in my lap, useless.

And then I'm thinking of her cabin. Of the screams, the smoke, the way the walls still smell of her. I swore I'd never go back, not after they dragged her out. But the memory claws at me. I need to feel her again, even if it hurts.

By the time I notice I've moved, I'm outside, feet dragging through leaves. Each step jerks another sob loose. The cabin waits through the trees like it's been waiting all along.

I collapse on the porch, forehead pressed to my knees, bawling until my ribs ache, until the wood under me is slick with tears and snot. I can't make myself go in.

CHAPTER 8
Echoes of Fire
Morgan

The door gave with a long scrape when I shoved it open.

The air inside was cold and stale, smoke pressed deep into the boards. Herbs dangled brittle from the rafters. A cracked mirror leaned against the wall; its face fractured into spiderweb lines. A quilt slouched over the chair by the hearth. In the corner, a wooden horse lay on its side, one ear broken clean off.

My boots groaned against the floorboards as I stepped farther in. Dust curled through the strip of light behind me.

That's when it started again.
The ache.

Low in my chest, dull at first, then sharper with every step forward.

I pressed my palm against my sternum, but it didn't ease.

And then the door slammed shut.

I spun, brushing my hilt, pulse climbing fast.

And she was there.

Joanna

The warped frame always made the door slam. I hadn't meant it to be that loud.

There was a woman; no, a Fae, standing in my mother's cabin. She turned at the sound, quick and dangerous. My throat went dry. Every story I'd ever heard about them came rushing back: Fae are killers. Fast and strong. Able to snap you like a twig before you blink.

My fingers tightened around the dagger until the grooves bit my palm. Her eyes moved over everything, Mama's quilt, the wooden horse, the mirror that cracked during the struggle. My life scattered and dusty, and she was standing in the middle of it like she belonged.

I stepped forward, the floor groaning under my weight.

"Don't move," I said, my voice shaking but steady enough.

Her head snapped toward me.

Morgan

She stood by the door, hood down, dagger drawn. Her eyes were sharp, locked on mine.

And I saw them, marks faint along her skin, glowing just enough no one else would notice. But I did.

She's a Witch.

My grip tightened on the hilt. Training hammered into me: draw, strike, end it.

But the ache flared in my chest, a sharp hand closing around my heart. I couldn't move.

The silence stretched, heavy and unbearable.

Then frost crunched outside. Footsteps.

"Morgan?"

Lena's voice. Relief hit so hard my knees almost went out. Thank the gods. She'd followed me into this "forest fire" after all.

The witch's eyes widened.

Joanna

Another voice outside. Female. Fae.

Morgan?

The name struck like a blow. My chest seized, ribs aching as if the word itself had claws.

My eyes snapped back to the Fae in front of me. "Morgan?" I rasped.

The name felt familiar, like it had been waiting on my tongue all along.

Morgan

The witch said my name like she already knew
it.

My chest burned hotter, the ache pressing so hard
it shook my breath.
How does she know me?
Who is she?

I didn't draw. I didn't move. I couldn't.

Her dagger trembled, but her eyes stayed locked
on mine.

Time stood still.

And the cabin held its breath.

CHAPTER 9
Splintered Silence
Joanna

I knew this. Fae.

Gods, it was Morgan. The one from my dreams. The name that still clung to my ribs like smoke. And now she stood here, dagger in hand, trespassing like she owned the place. Hunting witches as if I wasn't one.

Heat flushed up my throat, anger rising fast enough to mask the ache clawing at me.

The silence broke first.

"You don't belong here," I spat.

My throat was dry, my hand trembling around the dagger's hilt.
Steel hissed free in the cramped cabin.

Her voice was flat. "You don't belong anywhere, witch."

"This is my home, Fae."

Her gaze flicked to the cracked mirror, Mama's quilt slouched on the chair, the toy horse in the corner. And for a breath, just a flicker, her face shifted. A flinch. Small, but I saw it.

Then she straightened, cold again. "Well. It's filthy."

The words cut deeper than they should. I wanted to demand why she was here, why the dream had followed me into waking. Instead, all I could manage was: "Then get out."

Joanna

My fingers tightened around the dagger until the grooves bit my palm. Her eyes moved over everything, Mama's quilt, the wooden horse, the mirror that cracked during the struggle.

I stepped forward, the floor groaning under my weight. "Don't move," I said, my voice shaking but steady enough.

Her head snapped toward me.

Morgan

Her voice snapped, sharp, covering the tremor underneath.

I raised my blade. Training screamed to end it fast, leave no trace. My chest screamed to hold still.

"You're dangerous," I said. "I should end you now."

Her eyes narrowed, mocking even through the fear. "Then why haven't you, Fae?"

The heat in my veins snapped. I lunged. Steel clashed with hers, a crack loud enough to shake the walls.

Joanna

The impact jolted my wrist. She was stronger too strong, but I shoved back anyway, teeth clenched. Sparks flew as steel scraped steel.

Heat bled to my free hand, white and wild, light flaring at my fingertips before I could stop it.

"Get away from me!" I shouted and let it surge.

The blast struck her square in the chest. She flew backward, slammed into the wall with a bone-deep boom that rattled the rafters. Dust rained down in sheets.

I gasped, heart racing, my hand still humming with leftover heat. I hadn't meant to throw her that far. But still, why here? Why her?

Morgan

Pain snapped up my spine when I hit the wall. My blade clattered across the floorboards. I dragged it back to my hand, slick with blood. The air reeked of fire and salt.

I hadn't expected that kind of power from her. Stronger than she knew.

I forced myself upright, magic sparking instinctively down my arm, green-blue fire threading my veins.

"You don't even know what you're doing," I ground out. "Or how dangerous you are."

Her chest heaved, defiant. "Still dangerous enough to burn you."

I thrust my hand forward. Light flared from me, clean and controlled, snapping across the room.

Her fire met mine in the middle. Power smashed together, snarling against itself, until the cabin walls groaned with the shockwave.

Lena

The whole building shook. White light seared through the cracks in the boards, hot enough to sting.

"MORGAN!" I shouted, circling the cabin. "Answer me!"

Another crash. A muffled cry. Then silence.

My gut twisted tight. Something was very wrong.

Joanna

Her magic cracked like glass against mine. I shoved harder, letting the wildness take me. My fire tore through hers, unrelenting.

She flew again, crashing into the chair by the hearth. Wood splintered under her weight. Mama's quilt slid to the floor in a heap.

Her blood streaked down her temple, but still she pushed up, blade in hand, staggering but unbroken.

"Why won't you just fall?" I hissed.

Her voice came ragged but steady. "Because I can't."

Morgan

My ribs screamed. My knuckles split from gripping too tight. Blood slicked my temple, hot and sticky.

But she wasn't untouched. Sweat shone on her jaw, and a thin line of blood cut down her arm where my blade had grazed her. Still, she stood. Still, she burned.

I steadied my blade. "You're reckless. You'll destroy everything in this place."

Her lip curled. "Maybe that's what it deserves."

I blinked slow, biting back a grin despite the pain. "Didn't you just call it yours?"

Her glare could've pierced skin. She lifted her hand again, light pooling in her palm, the air heating fast.

I lunged.

Lena

The crash nearly split the frame. Sparks hissed from the seams of the cabin.

"MORGAN!"

No answer. Only more wood breaking, another ragged cry, another blast that scorched the air.

That was enough.

I drew my sword and slammed my boot into the swollen door. The frame groaned and splintered. I didn't stop until it gave way.

Joanna

The door flew open.

I spun, chest heaving, dagger raised in one hand, fire still burning in the other.

Another Fae filled the doorway, sword drawn, eyes wide.

Her gaze swept the wreckage, the scorched table, the shattered chair, the blood smeared on both of us.

She froze.

Morgan

Lena stood in the doorway, sword steady, eyes darting over the wreckage.

Me with my blade raised, blood dripping down my temple. The witch opposite me, fire burning in her palm, eyes locked on mine.

The cabin was wrecked. The tether burned hot under my ribs.

And I knew Lena was wondering why I hadn't finished it. Why the witch still stood.

CHAPTER 10
Splinters of Smoke
Lena

The door split under my boot, and I charged inside, sword high.

The cabin was wrecked. Smoke clung to the rafters. The table was split in two. A chair splintered to kindling. Herbs dangled brittle from the beams like dead birds. Ash drifted from the hearth in thin, gray threads.

96

And in the middle of it all, Morgan and the witch.

Both bloodied. Both shaking. Both standing like idiots instead of finishing it.

"Gods, Morgan! What the hell are you doing? You should've killed her already!"

I crossed the room in two strides and slammed the witch to the floor. My sword pinned her throat. Her dagger scraped against mine, the sound sharp enough to sting my teeth.

"Witch," I snarled. "What's your name?"

Her mouth twisted. "Why? So, you can kill me faster once you know it?"

Rage surged hot in my chest. "I'm not going to ask you twice."

Her eyes burned back into mine, unflinching.

"What, so you can hunt my family too? Too late. They're already dead."

The words hit harder than I wanted them to. My grip tightened until my knuckles ached.

Morgan

"Enough! Stop, Lena!"

I ripped the witch out of Lena's hold, fist twisted in her tunic. I slammed her against the wall, hard enough to rattle the boards. Her dagger clattered across the floor.

She gasped for breath, but her glare never faltered.

"What the fuck is your name?" I snarled, blade pressing against her collarbone.

Nothing. Her jaw locked tight.

I shoved harder, the ache in my chest spiking with each breath. "Say it!"

Her lips curved in something like a smile. "What, afraid you can't kill me without it?"

The pull inside me throbbed so fierce I could barely think. Rage told me to end it. Training told me to end it. But I couldn't move. Couldn't strike.

I looked for leverage. That's when I saw her eyes flick, just for a heartbeat, toward the quilt crumpled by the hearth. Not anger. Not hate. Something else.

Grief.

I snatched it up, fingers curling tight around the fabric. My free hand sparked, heat coiling until smoke lifted from the edge of the quilt.

Her composure cracked. A sharp gasp broke out of her.

"Don't," she whispered, raw.

I burned it hotter, the threads trembling under my palm.

"Then tell me your name."

Joanna

My chest locked so tight I thought I'd choke. Mama's quilt dangled from her hand like it was nothing, like it wasn't the last piece of her I had left.

Rage scalded through me. I wanted to spit in her face, to laugh, to die before I gave her the satisfaction.

But the smoke rose. Another second and it would catch. My throat broke before my will did.

"Joanna," I rasped. The word tasted like blood.

Morgan

The name hit me like a blade through the ribs.

Time stuttered. The ache under my sternum tore wide open, so raw I thought it would split me in two.

Jo.

I'd whispered the name in dreams.

Joanna.

The witch in front of me.

My grip shook. My blade hovered uselessly at her collarbone. Breath tore out of me, uneven, desperate. I couldn't move. Couldn't strike.

The silence in the cabin was heavier than any chain.

Lena

I saw it. All of it.

The way Morgan's face went pale. The way her hand trembled instead of cutting. The way that name hollowed her out.

Jo.

The one she'd refused to explain.

This witch. This girl.

The pieces slammed together like an axe hitting bone.

My sword stayed ready, but my hands hesitated for the first time in years. Not out of pity. Not out of fear. But because the way Morgan looked at her told me this was bigger than duty.

Dust drifted from the rafters. The only sound was our breathing, ragged and loud.

Three of us, caught in silence so tight, felt like the cabin was enclosing us.

CHAPTER 11
Fractures in the quiet
Lena

If the Court found us like this, we were finished. Done for. We'd be dead by morning.

I shoved past Morgan, rope already coiled in my hand. The cabin smelled of smoke and sweat, of burned herbs and something coppery under it. Splinters glittered on the floor like teeth. The witch's boots left dark prints in the ash.

"Next time you decide to commit treason, at least give me a heads-up," I said, deadpan, because sarcasm steadies the hand. "I might pack snacks." Then I jabbed the rope toward the witch. "Move, the witch needs tying now."

She didn't move at first. Just stared, eyes hollow and tired. Finally, she shifted, folding herself into the nearest motion as if every muscle had been drained. When I lunged, she didn't fight much; the fight was in her look.

"Afraid to kill me, so you tie me like an animal?" she sneered, voice flat and bitter.

"Shut your mouth." I yanked her wrists forward.

Rope bit skin; the twine bit back. Each knot I cinched made her hiss, breath scraping like paper against the wound. The fibers scraped my palms raw, but knots are practical; they don't care about poetry.

"Don't mistake our mercy for weakness," I said, quick, brittle. Let her think us kind. Let her think us sane.

She laughed, harsh, ragged. "Mercy? That's what you call waiting to decide which of you kills me?"

I bound her ankles to the splintered chair leg. The wood caught; the chair groaned and made a sound like something giving up. She glared at me, eyes hot with hatred, better than begging.

Hatred is honest.

I stood, blade heavy in my hand, and looked at Morgan. The ash dusted her hair. Her breathing was a ragged thing.

"If the Court hears of this, we're dead. You damned us the second you hesitated."

The words should have landed like an order. A threat. Steel. Instead, they felt like a confession. Even if the Court demanded I kill Morgan to save myself, I wasn't sure I could.

Morgan

Heat crawled up my neck as Lena tightened the last knot. The rope cinched the witch into place like a fang around bone. The cabin felt smaller, the air hotter, every breath a rough bargain.

I should've ended this. I had the training. The strike. The law on my side. I had all the reasons in the world to finish it clean and worth a damn. So why couldn't I? Why did this witch hold me like a snare instead of a target?

Joanna looked at me and saw the falter. She read the tremor on my fingers like a map. She marked it; she filed it away as weakness. Her eyes were small, hungry with something that wasn't just fear, something that recognized my hesitation and waited to use it.

The ache under my ribs was a drum. Each knot Lena tied beat against it, like a metronome counting out my inability.

I kept my blade up because you never drop your guard. But my hand shook. The edges of the world wavered with every breath.

Lena

I checked the knots again. Fingers quick, practiced.

"If she twitches, she'll bruise," I said, more to myself than to anyone.

The cold outside bit at my cheeks the second I crossed the threshold.

"I'll scout," I said. "If the Court finds us here, we'll be in chains before sunrise."

The words were blunt and hard as flint. I cast a last look back at Morgan, half-order, half-plea.

"You're on watch duty. Since you can't finish the job."

Saying it made my stomach twist; the venom in my voice was armor. Underneath, I was a mess. Her blade had trembled. I didn't know if my job was to protect her from the Court or the Court from her.

Dark swallowed the trees as I stepped away. Frost stung my nostrils. My boots left prints in the ash-slick path. The night felt loud, as if the world was holding its breath for us to fail.

Joanna

The cabin settled behind me. Rope burned at my wrists; I lifted my chin because that is what you do when someone ties you down, you keep your face soft as a threat.

"Watch duty, huh?" I said, the words sliding out before I could stop them. "You look like a hound waiting at the door."

She tensed in a way that almost looked like pain.

"You want me dead, but you can't even look at me," I said, softer.

A challenge, and a confession.

Her gaze snapped back to mine, and for a heartbeat, she looked like she hated herself more than she hated me. It was a quick thing, gone in a blink. But I saw it. It landed somewhere low in my ribs like a stone.

Morgan

She had a way of crawling under my skin with a single smirk.

"Shut up," I muttered.

She leaned forward against the ropes, smirking now. "Make me."

My eyes went wide. The fire in the hearth cracked like a punishment. This witch was going to make me pay for every second I hesitated.

Joanna

"So that's your thing then? Tie women up and stare at them?" I jabbed at the air with my chin.

Morgan's scowl cut sharp. "Better than burning them in the streets."

"Oh, so noble. Should I start singing ballads about you?"

"I didn't say that."

"No, really, what's your plan? Glare at me until I drop dead?"

"You're alive, aren't you?" she snapped.

"Oh, thank the gods. My savior. Should I kiss your boots now or later?"

She ground her teeth. Her mouth twitched a fraction; it was almost amusement. Almost.

112

Morgan

Gods help me; she was almost funny. Almost.

"You've got a sharp mouth for someone who can't move."

"Would you prefer I scream and bring your Court down on us?"

I dragged my hand down my face. "Please don't."

"Gods, you're impossible."

"Oh? Impossible's all you've got, Fae?"

I sighed, the blade lowering like a tired soldier. "Fine. Talk all you want. No one's listening."

"Oh, you're listening," she said, voice softer. "Otherwise, you'd have walked away or killed me already."

She was right. The thought knotted in my gut, and I didn't like where it pulled.

Her head tipped back, eyelids heavy. "You'll watch me anyway. Might as well sleep." The words were even, almost bored.

She settled like someone surrendering to a chair. The ropes held. The room stilled.

Morgan

The ropes kept her steady. For the first time tonight, she didn't seem like a threat, almost peaceful.

The ache under my ribs burned low and steady, a pulse I couldn't ignore.

The hearth crackled. She shifted, lips parting as sleep found her. The sound that escaped was small and soft—

"Mmm…Morgan…"

Breath hitched. Name folded around me. The syllables were slow, like honey sliding off a spoon.

My name, voiced in half-sleep, something intimate and private and not meant to be said aloud here, in this wreckage.

My hand went slack on the blade. Iron clattered. For a moment the world reduced to that sound, the name, thin as thread, loud as a bell. Her voice in dream dug its claws in. She was dreaming of me. Not of fear, not of fur; of me.

And then the tether answered.

It didn't grow slow or polite. It slammed through me, raw want with the gentle insistence of tide. It knotted around my sternum and pulled.

The want wasn't mine. It arrived from somewhere older, something hungry and sure. My breath hitched, my knees threatened to give. The blade felt useless; the rope felt useless.

The cabin spun. My vision narrowed to the little rise and fall of her chest, the soft sound of her sleeping breath, and the tether's hot pulse under my skin.

I held my ground all night. I had given orders, tensed like steel, felt righteous. The tether tore at all of that and left me exposed.

I leaned back against the cleft of the wall, palms pressed to my ribs as if to hold the thing in. The want thrummed, insistent and maddening. I could not command it. I could not name it. I could only feel the drag and the opening beneath it, the ache that felt suddenly like an answering call.

And in that silence, while the witch slept and the rope bit at her wrists, I realized the choice had already been made. The tether was for me.

CHAPTER 12
The Sound that undid me
Morgan

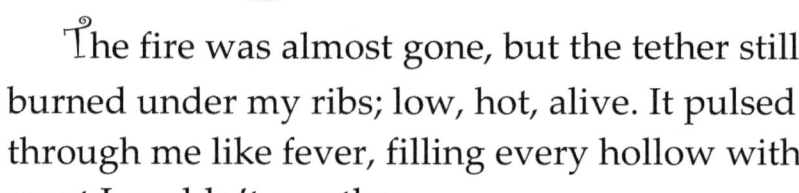

The fire was almost gone, but the tether still burned under my ribs; low, hot, alive. It pulsed through me like fever, filling every hollow with want I couldn't smother.

Every breath dragged her name out of me whether I meant it or not.

Jo.

Soft, quiet, like a curse or a prayer.

I tried pacing. Sharpening my knife. Counting the cracks in the rafters.

Nothing worked.

"Get it together, Morgan," I hissed under my breath. "She's just a witch. Yeah, she's hot. And she's all tied up. Stop, I can't keep thinking those thoughts. She's a witch. Literally, your sworn enemy."

The ache only clawed deeper. It coiled low in my stomach, crawling up my spine until I thought I'd choke on it.

Panic spiked. I dropped to my knees on the rug, forehead pressed into it like prayer might work on someone like me. My fingers fisted in the worn fibers.

"Jo," I whispered. "What are you doing to me? I can't stop. Why can't I make this stop?"

Behind me, the rope creaked. She shifted in the chair.

I froze.

Silence.

Then I started babbling again, faster, louder, like noise could drown the heat building in my chest.

"It's fine. Totally fine. Completely normal. She's not that attractive. She's infuriating, insufferable…"

"Talking to the floorboards?" she drawled, voice smug and sleepy.

Heat shot up my neck like a flare.

"I'd help you out," she added, that wicked grin audible in her tone, "but I'm all tied up."

"Oh, my gods; Jo!" I yanked my cloak over my head like a child hiding from a nightmare. "You heard that?" I muttered through the cloth.

Joanna

Oh, this was too good.

My terrifying fae captor kneeling on the rug, face buried in it, babbling my name like a guilty prayer. I couldn't help but tease her.

"Mmm… Morgan…" I moaned, long and low, letting it roll off my tongue like honey.
She flushed deeper, visible even in the dim firelight.

"Ohhh, Morgaaan…" I dragged it out, theatrical, hand to my chest for effect.

She actually bit the rug. Bit it.

"Oh, my gods," I laughed, clutching the armrest to keep from falling over. "You're making out with the rug!"

She whipped her head up, hair a mess, cloak half-tangled around her. "I wasn't…it's not like that…I didn't—"

Her voice broke in the last word, and that was it. I lost it. Laughter spilled out of me, bright and breathless.

Morgan

Dawn leaked pale through the cracks in the shutters. My head ached from holding in silence. Joanna stirred in the chair. Her hair tangled, wrists raw, that smug curl still stamped on her mouth.

"Well, well," she rasped. "Still on the rug? Isn't that where I left you?"

Heat flushed up my neck. "Do not."

Her grin sharpened. "You and Rug Daddy had a moment."

"Oh, my gods." I rubbed both hands down my face. "Please stop."

She hummed, pleased with herself. I briefly considered gagging her, then realized that would probably just make things worse.

122

Lena

The door slammed open under my boot so hard the hinges screamed. "We have to go. Now. The Court knows…"

The sentence died on my tongue.

The room hit me like a punch: Morgan flushed, half-crouched on the rug. Joanna tied to the chair, smirk lazy as sin.

"Gods damn it, Morgan." My voice cracked like a whip. "What the hell did you do?"

"Nothing!" she snapped, too quick, too defensive.

Joanna tilted her head, all mock innocence. "That's not what it sounded like last night."

"Shut up!" Morgan barked.

I could feel my blood pressure rising like a storm.

"You've lost your mind. Whatever this is, get control before the Court does."

My gaze flicked to the rug then to Morgan's face.
The meaning clicked in all the wrong ways. "Leave
her. We don't have time."

Morgan hesitated one heartbeat too long. Then she
rose, blade in hand, jaw tight, and followed me
out.
The door slammed behind us.

Joanna
   Silence swallowed the cabin whole.
The ropes dug deep into my wrists, raw skin
burning where they'd rubbed through the night.
Smoke and sweat clung to me like a second skin.
My throat hurt from laughing, from shouting,
from pretending none of this had touched me.

They'd left me. Tied. Forgotten.

   For a long moment, I just sat there, chest rising
and falling in shallow, furious breaths.
Rage burned hotter than shame.

Not just at Lena.
Not just at the rope.
But at Morgan.
She could've cut me free.
She didn't.
She left me.

If they thought leaving me humiliated would save them, fine. Let them think it.

They'd regret it soon enough.

CHAPTER 13
The Court Summons
Morgan

They didn't kill me that night.

Instead, they left me in the dark, no food, no light, just the slow drip of water and the stink of iron.

I counted the sounds to stay sane.

One drop. Two. Three.

By the third day, I stopped trying to tell time.

The air was thick enough to chew. Every breath scraped my throat raw. Rust flaked from the chains whenever I moved. My wrists were blistered, my mind frayed. The dark pressed close heavy and endless until I started whispering just to hear a voice. Any voice.

When they finally came for me, light burned like a weapon. The door split open; torches stabbed the dark.

They dragged me through the corridor with rough hands, clanking chains, the sour musk of armor and sweat. Stone scraped my knees when I hit the floor. The air smelled of incense and judgment.

They shoved me into the chamber like a corpse that hadn't realized it was dead.

Cold Stone. Torchlight glinting off metal. The sound of boots and silk and shallow breath. Every tier was full, every faction perched in its corner like predators scenting blood.

The Antlered sat rigid, antlers glinting, eyes steady and cold. The Hollow-born whispered like a nest of serpents, their hoods swallowing their faces. The Gilded fanned jeweled silks and smirked behind glassy smiles. The Dreadmarked lounged and laughed, tattoos crawling like smoke across their skin.

And there Zane among the Antlered, iron bands wound around his antlers, posture sharp as a blade. Kael tilted his mirrored mask from the Hollow tier, one blue eye-catching torchlight. Ciaran lounged with the Dreadmarked, flame-bright hair and a grin sharp enough to draw blood. The Hollow hissed louder. Chains jerked against my arms. I smiled anyway.

"Bring the witness," a voice commanded.
Boot steps echoed.

My stomach dropped.

Oh no, Lena.

They dragged her forward, forced her to kneel opposite me. Her shoulders were square, her gaze fixed forward, but she didn't look at me.
Ciaran leaned forward, grin wicked. "Ah, one of ours. Tell us, sweet Dreadmarked — what did you find in the cabin?"

Her jaw clenched. "We tracked together. I lost her in the forest. That's all I remember."

Kael's voice cut in, smooth as water, sharp as glass. "Say it plain. You know I'll see the lie."

And he would. Seer always saw what wasn't meant to be seen.

The chamber stilled.

Lena's eyes flicked to me, just once. Quick. Pained. Then she said it.

"The witch was tied to a chair. Morgan was on the floor. Her face crimson. And the witch told me, 'That's not what you did last night.'"

Her voice didn't shake. Mine almost did.

"There's a first time for everything, I guess," she added, tone brittle. "Usually she just ruins missions, not careers."

The chamber erupted. Gasps. Jeers. Whispers slicing like blades. Even the Dreadmarked spat.

"She reeks of her," sneered a Gilded.

"Bound herself to filth," hissed a Hollow.

Ciaran laughed loud enough to shake the torches.

"One of mine; dragging back a feral fae who tangles herself in witch scent. Charming."

I yanked at my chains. "That's not...I didn't even touch..."

"SILENCE!"

The doors opened.

Erelith swept in, jeweled cuffs flashing. The Gilded rose as one, silks whispering, jeers sharpening in his wake. His eyes slid from Lena to me, mouth curving slow.

"The soldier confirms it."

My teeth ground together.

"She confirmed I'm alive. Great work. Maybe next you'll solve fire is hot."

A hiss cut the air. The Gilded didn't appreciate humor.

Erelith's smile turned thin.

"Morgan of the Wilds. You reek of a witch. You are tainted. And the Court does not forgive filth."

The factions roared; Antlered pounding their spears, Hollow whispering like floodwater, Gilded snapping silks.

I turned to Lena. "Hope they wrote you a good script. That lie was almost believable."

Her jaw locked. Her gaze dropped.
Erelith flicked a jeweled hand, bored.

"Contain her. She will prove useful later."

Hands seized me. Chains bit deep. They dragged me backward through the roar of voices.

Ciaran clapped twice, slow and mocking.
Zane stayed stone still, but his eyes followed me.

The last thing I saw before the doors slammed was Lena's face steel everywhere but her eyes.

And I thought:
If I'm going down, at least I'll go down loud.

Joanna

The ropes cut deeper the harder I fought.
Wrists raw. Shoulders screaming. My breath tore in and out through clenched teeth.

I shoved harder. The chair tipped, crashed. My head smacked the floor, teeth rattling. Splinters stabbed my cheek.

"Perfect," I muttered into the boards. "Why wouldn't I face-plant in my mother's grief cabin? Gold star."

I rocked, again and again, until the leg joint groaned. A weak spot. I twisted and pulled until the wood cracked loud enough to echo. My wrist tore free. Blood slicked my hands. The rest came undone under shaking fingers.

I stood, dizzy, breath ragged, wrists bleeding. The dagger slid back into my palm like it had missed me.

They thought they could leave me to rot. They'd pay for that.

I stepped into the frost, cloak snapping in the wind, and followed the trail north.

The tether hummed faint under my ribs, faint, but there. Pulling me toward something I didn't understand and couldn't ignore.

Morgan

The guards hooked me high, arms stretched until my shoulders screamed. Chains bit bone. My toes barely touched the floor.

Boots scraped. Keys jingled. The smell of perfume curled through the damp.

Ines entered like she owned the air calm, deliberate, her pale robes moving like smoke.

"My little star," she purred, thumb grazing my chin. "They've been unkind."

Her fingers pinched my jaw just enough to sting, then softened, tracing the same spot with a feather touch.

It was always like that hurt, then soothe. A lesson disguised as affection.

"Good," she murmured, smile too sweet. "I'll see you later."

She winked, turned, and the guards' laughter filled the void she left.

They hit harder this time, fists to my ribs, boots to my gut, and a yank on the chain until my shoulder popped.

They chewed meat in front of me, spat gristle at my feet.

"Drink the damp, fae filth."

By the time they left, I hung limp, blood in my mouth, breath shallow.

I didn't dare close my eyes. Sleep brought dreams, and dreams brought her voice, you're mine.

That was worse than the pain.

Joanna

Tracking her was almost easy.

135

Broken branches. Faint blood smears. Deep footprints where her body had been dragged.

And that pull low and sharp, like a thread stitched through my ribs, tugging north.

By nightfall, torchlight flickered through the trees. The air was alive with wards glowing sigils burning across the perimeter, humming like hornets.

I dropped low, breath shallow. Guards clomped past, armor heavy, steps out of rhythm. The smell hit me first. Iron. Rot. Damp.

Chains rattled somewhere ahead. A sound like bone grinding stone.

I followed it. The closer I got, the tighter the tether pulled until it was a knife in my chest. I was close.

A hand shot from the shadows and yanked me down.

Kael

The witch hit stone hard, knife flashing.
Zane caught her wrist before she could strike. His
grip didn't budge. "I wouldn't."

"She's not one of ours," he muttered.

"She is," I said, stepping from the dark.

The threads glowed around her, silver-bright,
pulled taut toward the one chained below.

"The weave put her here."

She spat at my boots. "You don't know me."

"I don't," I said. "But I see you. You came for her.
To kill her."

Her silence was the answer.

Zane's jaw flexed.

"Fine," he said low. "But if you twitch wrong, I'll
end you."

Joanna

Torches guttered low, shadows crawling. The air inside reeked of damp and iron. My boots barely whispered, but my heartbeat thundered.

And then, I saw her.

Morgan.

Chains hauled her high, arms stretched raw. Bruises bloomed along her ribs. Cuts crusted with blood. Her head sagged, lips cracked, skin too pale.

I should've felt satisfaction. She'd left me tied and humiliated.

Instead, my stomach turned.

She looked small.

I stepped closer, the iron scent hollowing my chest. "Gods... Morgan. What did they do to you?"

Her head jerked weakly. Eyes cracked open, cloudy and bright all at once. They found me. Unsteady. Disbelieving.

"Jo...?"

My knees went weak. Tears blurred my sight. Zane's blade flashed. The chain split. She fell dead weight, and I caught her before she hit stone.

Her cheek pressed to my shoulder, wet with blood and heat.

"We don't have time," Zane said.

"Rumors are already spreading," Kael murmured.

I didn't move. Couldn't.

Morgan leaned heavy against me, breath tearing raw, and for the first time since the fire, I felt whole.

Morgan

Chains gave way one snap, one heartbeat —
and I fell.

Would've cracked my skull if Jo hadn't caught me.
Gods, she was warm.

Her arms shook but held. Her cheek pressed to
my hair, damp and hot with tears. I tried to say
something clever, maybe flirt with death again, but
all that came out was a wheeze. Smooth. Really
impressive.

Jo didn't move. Just looked at me like she saw
something fragile instead of feral. I hated it. Hated
how her eyes burned through me.
Then she shifted, slung me onto her back like I
weighed nothing, and cinched me there with her
sword belt.

My wrists locked around her neck. My face
pressed to her shoulder. Her hair smelled like
smoke and pine and sin.

140

Boot steps thundered. Torches flared. The alarm screamed through the hall.

Zane shoved us into an alcove, his antlers scraping stone as a patrol stormed past.

I tried to hold my breath. Tried not to cough.

Failed spectacularly.

Instead, I buried my face against her neck. Mistake. Too close. Too much heat. My heart skipped and stuttered.

At the far wall, Kael pressed a palm to the stone. The rock groaned and split open, cold air spilling through.

"Out. Now."

Zane pushed us through first.

Night slammed into us sharp and freezing. I sucked it in like salvation. The frost tasted sweet after weeks of damp.

And still, strapped to her back, breathing her in, I thought:

If I die here, at least I'm strapped to a gorgeous witch because gods damn it, she's hot.

CHAPTER 14
Zane's Oath
Zane

(The Antlered do not speak. They remember.)

Elk-femur spears tipped in ash slammed the floor, every strike a heartbeat.

A reminder: **we are never still.**

Smoke curled up from the torches, painting antlers in gold and shadow. The rhythm shook the stone beneath us. I felt it crawl through my ribs, into the marrow of my spine, the old war pulse.

Iron bands clamped around my antlers, carved with resin-dark runes from the day they sealed me.

The elders crooned as they set them:
This gives you loyalty. Restraint. Silence.

Among the Antlered, restraint is strength. Noise is weakness. A true stag stands silent until the strike. My silence was an oath as much as the iron.

And gods, the iron was heavy.

But silence couldn't still my heart when they dragged her out in chains.

Morgan.

Light as smoke, all sharp edges and wild eyes, a spectacle for them to shred. The Court smelled blood; they wanted a story, a scapegoat, a beast they could cage and call justice.

They called her *feral. Tainted.*

But when she stood there stone-faced, steady, fire buried under her ribs she didn't look like a monster. She looked like someone refusing to kneel.

Most fae beg or spit. She did neither.

She reminded me of myself.

We, the Antlered, believe every soul carries a tether veins to soil, blood to bark. Before battle, we press our foreheads to dirt, lower our antlers, vow to return unbroken.

Break the tether, and you lose your way. Wander too far, and the forest forgets your name. The elders hammered iron into me young.

Painted soot across my chest.

Ran me until my hooves split and my lungs tore.

They taught me how to carry the herd's weight.

How to bleed for them.

How to obey.

But they never taught me what to do when obedience looked like cruelty.

The Herd-Prayer rolled through the chamber, a low hum of devotion:
Guide us through the dirt.
The ancient one seeks your trust.

Around me, they mouthed the vow in unison:
Run silent. Strike true. Return as one.

I mouthed it too, ash bitter on my tongue. My brother, Thalos, sat two tiers above, his eyes like whetted knives. To him, hesitation was rot. Weakness. If he saw my fear for Morgan, he'd carve it out of me and call it mercy.

The oath the elders bound to me trembled under her light. I felt it crack. Gleam. Change shape.

So, I made another promise, the kind you carve into bone so it can't be taken back.

I pressed my palms to the bands until the metal bit skin, until the runes hissed warm.
Quietly, so the herd would never hear because the Antlered don't *break* oaths.

We carve new ones.

Bone against bone.

I swore not to the herd.
Not to the hunt.
To her.

Run silent.
Strike true.
Return as one.
And when I mouthed *one,* it was for Morgan.

The iron pulsed once faint, like a heartbeat trying to answer mine.

The runes flared ember-bright, then sank black again.

None of the herd stirred, but the air had shifted.
It was listening.

My private oath sat heavier than the bands on my skull.

It was a weight I could hold.
But it changed the shape of the hunt.
The memory of the herd's chant followed me into the dark
a low, endless drum.

Run silent. Strike true. Return as one.
Only this time, the rhythm wasn't theirs.
It was mine.

Chapter 15
The Run and Arrival
Joanna

Morgan was basically dead weight strapped to my back my very own ethereal, sarcastic backpack of bruises and bad decisions.

Every step I took was a fight.

Every breath felt like hauling guilt uphill.

"Keep moving," Zane said, low and steady the kind of tone that assumed obedience. The kind of tone I wanted to punch in the throat.

Of course, Antler Boy would talk like that.

Typical.

"Wow," I huffed, adjusting Morgan higher on my shoulders. "Do you always practice sounding like a walking tree, or were you born that way?

And unless those antlers double as a stretcher, I don't see you helping."

From the shadows, Kael bent into view, all smooth voice and sharper edges. "You could thank him, witch. You'd be lost without us."

"I wouldn't be lost," I shot back. "Just… creatively detoured. You haven't even seen my tracking skills."

He smiled that unnerving, too-knowing smile of his.
"Oh, I've seen plenty. That's what worries me."

The woods pressed close. The frost was heavy on every branch, the air cold enough to bite skin raw. Moss stuck to my boots; every exhale fogged the night.

Zane lifted two fingers.

We froze.

No words. No breath. Just instinct.

That's how he commanded not with noise, but with the kind of stillness that made the air obey.

Low voices drifted through the trees Hollow patrol. Torchlight bled through the frost, smearing gold against bark.

The light crept toward my face.
Too close. Too bright.

My heart slammed against my ribs, desperate and loud. If they found us now, we'd be pyre ash before dawn.

Morgan stirred, soft sound against my neck. I clamped a hand over her mouth before she could speak. Her hair brushed my cheek, warm against the cold, and gods, it didn't help.

Boots drew closer. Torchlight flared.
One more step, and we were done.

Then…
Zane snapped his fingers.

A deer burst from the brush, crashing through the undergrowth.

The patrol shouted, torches flailing as they ran after it.

Silence slammed back down like a dropped blade.

I didn't breathe again until the forest swallowed them whole.

My chest heaved. "I'm going to die of a heart attack before I ever get burned on a pyre."

Zane arched a brow, unimpressed, and motioned us onward. Sympathy clearly wasn't part of the antler code.

The trees thinned. The frost deepened. Every shadow felt too awake.

A branch cracked ahead; clean, deliberate. Not animal.

Zane's hand went to his blade.

Then he stepped out.

Hood up, tattoos crawling like inked serpents beneath his skin, Dreadmarked through and through.

I knew the type.

And I knew enough to hate the type.

"Fantastic," I muttered. "Because what this party needed was one more broody nightmare with an ego."

He shoved his hood back, grin wide enough to hurt.

"Well, well. Antler Boy brooding, Shadow Boy lurking, and a witch hauling her half-feral girlfriend around like a sack of potatoes. What a circus."

"She's not my girlfriend!" I snapped.

Ciaran arched a brow. "Sure, sweetheart. And I'm a celibate monk. Lies are fun. Keep going."

On my shoulder, Morgan groaned, voice rough, cracked, but still laced with that maddening humor.

"Bossy looks good on you."

I nearly dropped her. "Are you *kidding me*?"

Ciaran's grin sharpened. "See? Even your girlfriend agrees."

The tattoos along his neck pulsed faintly, like the ink itself was laughing.

Zane's antlers caught the moonlight like blades. "Leave," He ordered.

Ciaran just leaned against a tree, unbothered. "Not a chance, my broody deer prince. You've got Creepy Shadow Man, Half-Feral Fae, and a witch with trust issues. You need me. I'm the comic relief. And obviously…" he smirked, "the handsome one."

155

Kael sighed from behind his mask. "God's help us."

Before I could retort, Morgan's weight shifted her body sagged, heavy and limp.

"Shit…Morgan?!"

I dropped to my knees, cradling her against the moss. Her lashes fluttered once, then went still.

Even Ciaran's grin faltered. "Well… that doesn't look good."

"Incredible healer's insight," I snapped.

Zane crouched beside me, voice clipped and soldier-flat. "She's alive. Starved."

Kael pressed two fingers to her neck. Shadows curled like smoke around his wrist.

"Barely holding. She won't if we waste time."

A tense beat hung in the cold.

Then Ciaran flopped backward with a sigh.

"Guess it's official."

"What is?" I demanded.

"Your girlfriend's our problem now too."

"She's not..." I started, but Morgan stirred. Her lips curved, that familiar half-smile tugging the corner of her mouth.

"Eat," I snapped, shoving bread into her hand.

She stared at it like it had personally offended her.

"Bread is sadness pressed into shape."

"Eat it anyway."

Her gaze lifted, hazy but deliberate. "Gods, you're gorgeous."

I groaned. "Delirium's not cute on you."

"Delirium's not cute on anyone." Her lips curved again. "But you're still hot."

Ciaran laughed loud enough to scare birds from the trees.

"Are you two *seriously* doing this here?"

Kael didn't even look up. "Let them. The tension's unbearable."
The two of them fist-bumped like absolute children.

"You're children!" I hissed.

Morgan tilted her head, voice soft but unrelenting. "You're hot when you're flustered."

Heat crawled up my throat, my pulse thundering. "Stop talking."

Her smile was a knife she knew how to use. "Make me."

She leaned closer, lips ghosting the air between us. "With your mouth."

And gods...

I hated how much I wanted to.

CHAPTER 16
Firelight and Antlers
Joanna

The fire cracked and spat like it had opinions. Every pop sounded judgmental.

Ciaran hummed some tuneless disaster under his breath, part ballad, part noise complaint against the night, which somehow made everything *louder*.

The forest was too still, too listening.

Morgan slumped against me, limp and pale, her head heavy on my shoulder.

She looked like a corpse that occasionally busted out sarcasm.

I shoved a crust of bread against her lips. "Eat more."

She coughed, chewed with exaggerated suffering.

"If I die," she rasped, "let it be known the carbs finished me."

"Drama queen."

Across the fire, Zane muttered without looking up.
"She needs meat."

I raised a brow. "Oh? Do the antlers help you diagnose patients now?"

"They give me eyes," he said flatly.

161

I blinked. "Your antlers give you *eyes*?"

He rubbed his temple like I'd caused a migraine. "No. I have eyes to *see* she's weak. Strength doesn't come back on crumbs alone."

Ciaran lay sprawled on the moss, hands behind his head, grin already cocked.

"Listen to Antler Boy. He's actually right this time. But careful, if you let him talk too long, he'll start beating his chest and scaring squirrels to prove his manliness."

He sat up, puffing out his chest, lowering his voice to a ridiculous rumble.

"Me man. You woman. You listen to me."

Zane's jaw flexed. "This coming from a drunken dreadheaded fool."

Ciaran gasped, all mock offense. "Oh, those are fighting words."

162

He hopped to his feet, swaggering forward like an overgrown toddler who'd discovered testosterone.

Zane didn't even move. Just looked up, calm as stone which somehow made it worse.

Kael's voice cut through, smooth and sharp as glass.
"Enough. No sense arguing when we're all hungry."

The silence afterward wasn't peace it was the kind that pressed in on you. The kind that knew something was wrong.

Both their gazes flicked toward Morgan's shallow breaths, then away again, like it hurt to look too long.

"I'll hunt," Zane said finally, quiet but final.

163

Ciaran clapped his hands together, breaking the tension.

"And I'll go with you. Someone needs to make sure you don't accidentally impale yourself on those majestic horns. Besides, broody boys shouldn't wander off alone , they get sad and poetic."

Kael tilted his mask slightly, shadows whispering at its edge. "I'll stay. Someone should look after the girls. And Morgan needs more than a soldier's guilt to keep her alive."

I bit back a retort. I could handle it.
But… another set of eyes wasn't the worst thing in the world.

Zane rose, movements deliberate, heavy with that quiet power that always made the air shift. For a heartbeat, his gaze flicked from me to Morgan, lingering just long enough to sting. Then his hand brushed the hilt at his hip.

"We won't be long."

Ciaran gave a mock salute, grin wicked. "Off we go, into the dark with Mr. Deer Prince. What could possibly go wrong? If we die, bury me somewhere dramatic."

He twirled his dagger once, whistling a tune as he followed Zane into the trees.

Zane

The forest swallowed sound whole.
Even our breathing felt too loud.

The air smelled of damp earth, pine, and distant smoke. Unfortunately, my companion smelled like trouble and bad decisions.

"So," Ciaran drawled, ducking a branch, "were you born this broody, or did something tragic happen? Lost a bet? Killed a flower with your glare?"

I ignored him. Rabbit tracks. Fresh.
He didn't deserve the satisfaction of a reply.

"Dead parent?" he kept on. "Betrayed lover? Raised by wolves? No... elk. Definitely elk. Explains the horns."

I exhaled through my nose.

"None of the above. And being quiet doesn't make me less attractive than you."

His head whipped around. "You did *not* just say that."

"I was raised on a farm," I said evenly. "Herded animals. Brothers."

He blinked. "Farm?"

"Elk Boy has jokes," I said. "Goats. Chickens. The geese were demons."

Ciaran burst out laughing loud, wild, alive in a way the woods weren't.

"Oh, gods. I can see it now baby Zane, antlers glinting, running from a goose. This is the best day of my life."

"Laugh all you want," I muttered. "Geese bite harder than you fight."

He laughed harder, nearly tripping into a thorn bush. "I might actually like you, Antler Boy."

I grunted. "Don't."

For a while, the quiet was easy steps in rhythm, the frost crunching underfoot, our breath fogging together.

Then his tone shifted, just a hair softer.

"When I was ten," he said, pulling up his sleeve, "these marks showed up. Whole arm lit like someone branded me from the inside. The village kids called me snake-boy. Said I was cursed. Threw rocks."

I glanced at him, surprised at the honesty tucked between the jokes.

He smirked faintly. "I told them I'd eat them in their sleep."

I almost smiled. "Did you?"

"Nah. Didn't get the fangs. Poor me. Picked last in 'jump the creek.'"

The quiet returned, heavier now.

"My brothers weren't better," I said finally. "Didn't matter how hard I trained, how much I gave, it was never enough."

He looked at me sideways, grin softening. "Guess that means we both have baggage."

Ciaran

The underbrush rattled.

We froze.

A growl rolled low through the trees deep, hungry, close.

"Please be a rabbit," I whispered.

Zane almost smiled. "Definitely not a rabbit."

The boar burst out of the dark, tusks flashing white in the torchlight.

Zane moved first with his sword up, stance perfect, like a painting of heroism come to life. He probably practiced that pose when no one was watching.

I darted to the side, dagger in hand, heart thundering and grin wide, because if I was about to die, I might as well die *smug*.

The beast lunged. Its tusks scraped Zane's ribs and he didn't even flinch. Show-off.

"Gods above!" I shouted, circling. "It's like fighting an angry boulder!"

"Flank it," he barked.

And for once, I didn't argue. I darted left, whistled sharp. The boar turned, charging me like the idiot it was.

Zane's blade sang. One clean strike.
The creature collapsed with a wet, final thud.

Silence swept back in.

I bent over, panting. Then I started laughing.

"See? We make a great team! You stab things; I look amazing doing it. Balance."

Zane actually chuckled short, low, and probably against his will. "You nearly got trampled."

"And you nearly got skewered," I countered. "Balance."

He cleaned his blade, movements precise, ritualistic. But the corner of his mouth twitched. Just enough to count.

Gotcha.

We hefted the kill together, dragging it through the frost. The quiet wasn't awkward anymore just steady.

Breathing, moving, alive.

I glanced over, grin sly. "Gods, I think I'll keep you."

He sighed, resigned. "You talk too much."

"And you don't talk enough," I shot back. "Perfect match."

He didn't answer, but for a heartbeat, his shoulders eased and that was answer enough.

CHAPTER 17
The Crossing
Joanna

The fire cracked low, shadows bending long, stretching across the moss like they wanted to eavesdrop.

Kael sat across from us, still as carved bone, shadows curling lazy around his boots like he was listening without ears.

Morgan.

Gods, Morgan.

That mouth.

She was sprawled on the moss like some half-broken saint, half-feral, half-divine her hair spilling wild, lashes heavy, a bruise already blooming across her jaw. Even wrecked, she glowed like the world's most frustrating miracle.

I wanted…

No. Gods, Jo, get it together. She's gorgeous because she's fae. That's all. That's it.
But the way she kept looking at me made my ribs ache like she'd reached in and twisted them.

"Stop looking at me like that," I snapped.

Her lips twitched, faint smile cutting sharp.

"Why? You're not the one starving. Besides…" she tilted her head, voice going soft and cruel at once, "if I die, I want a beautiful point of view."

Heat crawled up my throat. "You're not going to die. You're dramatic. And delirious."

Her lashes fluttered, mouth curling wicked, daring.

"Admit it. You want to come closer."

The words gutted me.

Of course I wanted to.

Of course I wanted to close the distance, to press my palm to her throat just to prove she was real. But she was delirious. She didn't know what she wanted.

And she'd left me in that damned cabin to die.

Still,

Gods, the way she stared at my mouth like she remembered every dream we'd ever had

And I couldn't stop staring at hers.
Her mouth. Right there.
I could…

No. I can't. Gods, Morgan, what are you doing to
me?

I curled my fists tight until my nails bit
half-moons into my palms. I wasn't going to move.
I wasn't going to lean in.

The tether flared hot under my ribs anyway, a
pulse so deep it stole my breath.

I froze. Of course she saw.
Her grin went slow and wicked.
Heat flushed my neck. I wanted to die right there.

Across the fire, Kael's voice drifted, bone-dry:
"Should I leave you two alone?"

Gods. Kael's still here. I forgot he was here.
I buried my face in my hands, groaning.

When I finally looked up again, the
forest itself had changed.
Shadows stretched taller, bending strange. The
carved sigils in the trees pulsed faintly blue,

breathing like they were alive.
The air pressed heavy. My lungs caught.

And then…

CRACK.

A twig split.

My head whipped so fast my neck popped.
A small squirrel sat on a branch, tail flicking.

I laughed, half-hysterical. "Seriously? That's it?
Just a squirrel."

It tilted its head, chittered once.

Then it launched.
Straight at Morgan.

Morgan

For half a heartbeat, its shape warped, fur splitting
into fingers, claws long and wrong. My chest
seized.

No. No. No.

It's her.

The smell hit first: smoke and iron, sweet perfume curling thick in my lungs.
A voice slid through the air, velvet and knives.

You're mine, little pet.

My throat collapsed. Every breath turned jagged. Sweat slicked my skin.
I shoved backward, heels digging into moss, clawing for distance that didn't exist.

My body wouldn't obey. My limbs locked. The air vibrated.
Legs jerking. Arms trembling. Useless fists.

"Get off me—get off me—get off—"

The scream tore out of me raw, scraping my throat open.
Sound ricocheted through the trees. The world tilted.

Kael moved instantly.
His hand hovered near his dagger but his

eyes…gods, his eyes…knew.
He saw *her* in the shape of my fear.

All I could manage was a strangled whisper:
"Don't."

The squirrel blinked.

Fur again. Tail curling smug.

It scampered off into the dark as if nothing had
happened.

But the ghost of her touch stayed.
Her claws were still in my skin, in my bones.
The whisper coiled behind my ear like a curse that
wouldn't fade.

My belly ached, the tether throbbing
deep, like something inside me wanted to split
open.

I tried to breathe.
Only shards came out.

Joanna

Morgan shoved herself backward, wild-eyed, gasping.

"Morgan? Are you okay?"
I grabbed her shoulders. "It's okay, Hun. It's just a squirrel."

Her body shook hard enough to rattle my own.

Gods, she was terrified, really terrified, and I hated how my pulse jumped at the contact.

Holding her like this, feeling her tremble, something hot and ugly twisted low in me.

Then the forest shifted.

The sigils carved into the trees glowed, one after another, blue light spreading like veins. The shadows hissed. The air split.

Crows burst screaming from the canopy, hundreds of them, the sound so loud it scraped the sky.

And then…

The woods *exploded* with noise.

Ciaran barreled into the clearing first, dragging the leg of a massive boar, grin wider than sin.

"Guess who's eating good tonight!"

Zane followed, the other end slung over his shoulder, blood slick on his arm, antlers catching in the branches.

Ciaran beamed like a child who'd brought home chaos for dinner.

"Antler Boy here gutted the whole beast like a legend—lunging and pirouetting like a ballerina dodging tusks. It was majestic."

"Shut up," Zane muttered. But he wasn't really mad.

Kael didn't even blink. "You're bleeding on the moss."

"I'm seasoning it," Ciaran said, unbothered.

I just sat there, stunned the almost-kiss, the squirrel, the crows, the boar, and now these two idiots acting like lifelong friends.
This realm was officially cursed.

And through it all, Morgan still shook beneath my hands silent, trembling, her eyes darting toward the trees like the nightmare hadn't left.

CHAPTER 18

After the crossing

Joanna

The fire cracked low, shadows

The woods felt like they were holding their breath.
Even the wind had gone still, caught in the teeth of the branches above us.

We'd eaten the boar the boys dragged back, meat seared over Kael's slow-turning spit, fat popping into the flames, but the taste sat like ash in my mouth.

Across the fire, Morgan still leaned against me, trembling like a leaf in a storm. She looked wrecked, pale and feral, yet somehow still managing to look smug about it.

"You're still shaking," I said, sharper than I meant.

She gave the smallest nod. Then, out of nowhere, she pointed, eyes wide, almost feral.

"I think the squirrel cursed me."

I blinked. "…what?"

Her hair clung damp to her cheeks, tear-tracks cutting through dirt, but she still gave a wicked smile.

"You didn't see it? All judgmental. Beady little creepy eyes. Tail way too fluffy. Suspiciously fluffy."

I snorted. "So, you're saying the squirrel was evil?"

"Of course. Trained. A mythical magical find. Possibly immortal."

She croaked it like a dying queen, clutching an imaginary chest wound.

From across the fire, Ciaran barked out a laugh so loud it startled the crows in the branches.

"Wait, you panicked over a squirrel? Gods, that's too good!"

Morgan's head snapped toward him, slow and dangerous. "Not just any rodent. *The* rodent. …Bum… bum… bum."

Zane raised a brow. "Oh, you're serious?"

"Yeah, and she's also a little crazy," Ciaran added.

Morgan turned back to me, ignoring them all. "If I die by squirrel, promise me you'll give a eulogy that says it was something cooler. Like a razor-sharpened beast. Or a sentient pinecone."

I rolled my eyes. "You're exhausting. And there you go being all dramatic again."

"And yet," she whispered, and reached up to tuck a lock of my hair behind my ear. "You're still here. How brave."

Her fever-bright eyes caught mine. My pulse jumped.

Gods, I'm in for it. Morgan is feral, but she does know how to flirt.

Kael

I shifted closer to Zane and Ciaran, lowering my voice until the crackle of the fire almost swallowed it.

"The squirrel she keeps joking about…"

They both went still.

"It's not a squirrel," I murmured. "It was Ines."

They shut up.

"She found her," I added quietly, "and wanted her to know she was coming."

For a moment the fire cracked, and no one breathed. Then Ciaran forced a laugh too loud, and Zane just stared off into the distance, jaw hard as stone.

Morgan

I twirled a twig in my hand, forcing a smile back onto my face. My hands shook, but I spun the twig like a baton.

"Hear ye, hear ye, come one, come all. I hereby claim and pledge my service as old master of the Order of Anti-Squirrel Defenders!"

Jo huffed a laugh and elbowed me.

Across the fire, Ciaran bellowed, "Gods, she's unhinged."

Zane huffed. "You're not wrong."

And for a blissful moment, everything felt right. For a heartbeat, my laugh sounded like it belonged to me again.

Joanna

Gods, Morgan is unhinged. But under the bravado, I could still feel the tremor in her frame where she leaned into me. This humor is fun and games, but she had just been shaking from a supposed squirrel attack, eyes wide as glass.

Now she's muttering about vendettas and raccoons with fangs, and the boys just laugh.

I looked at them. Kael gave me a knowing look one small flick of his eyes that said *this isn't a joke.*

My stomach knotted.

I knew this wasn't about a squirrel at all.
What is this? What's going on?
Why did Morgan panic like that?

Lena

The summons chamber still burned behind my eyes, the laughing, the spitting, the chains, and the moment I tried to cover it with a lie. Morgan, my poor best friend. She just had to get dragged off like that. I hated doing it. Why would they make me? I might as well have stuck the dagger in her myself.

Now I was out here, obeying Court orders to "find" her, when the truth was I didn't want to find her for them at all. I wanted to make sure she was okay.

That's when I heard the sound. Not a loud scream, but sharp, muffled, like someone fighting in a dream. I froze.

189

Then laughter, Morgan's laugh, brittle and breaking. And the witch's voice after, trying too hard to sound steady.

I crept closer. Through the branches, firelight flickered. I saw them huddled close, Morgan shaking, Joanna holding her upright, the others pretending it was all some ridiculous squirrel joke.

But I saw Morgan's hand clawed at her chest like something had tried to rip its way out. That wasn't laughter.
That was survival dressed up as banter.

My stomach twisted. I wanted to rush in, blade drawn, demand answers. Instead, I stayed in the shadows, jaw clenched so hard it hurt. Because I already knew what the Court would say if they saw this. Witch. Taint. Burn them both.

I pressed my fist to my mouth, shaking. I'd damned her once already in the chamber. And now watching her lean into the witch like the tether itself might snap if she let go

I knew I couldn't damn her again.

"Gods forgive me," I whispered into the dark.
"Because Morgan, I can't save you."

CHAPTER 19
The Art of Almost
Morgan

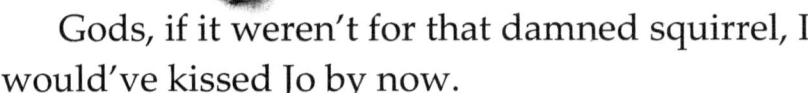

Gods, if it weren't for that damned squirrel, I would've kissed Jo by now.

I'd stopped shaking, but the panic still clung like smoke under my skin.
Joking about the squirrel was easier than admitting it had been *Ines*.

Easier than admitting I had trauma.

So, I kept twirling my stick, carving lines into the dirt, covering cracks with humor until Jo's face faltered.

"You know that squirrel almost had me," I said. "Could've executed me on the spot. Admit it, you'd miss me."

She glared, eyes flaring like struck flint. "It wasn't a squirrel, Morgan. *Admit* that."

The gut punch landed square. How did she know? How *could* she?

I bit down the tremor and spat venom to cover it. "Keep telling yourself that, witch. At least I can laugh. Hope you sleep well knowing you killed the humor."

Her hands shot up, fisting my tunic. She yanked me close, eyes inches from mine, voice a hiss. "Call me 'witch' one more time, and you'll find out just how dangerous I can be."

The tether burned hot under my ribs. My pulse rattled, everything tightening in my chest.

Then—

"What the hell are you doing, Morgan?!"

Lena's voice tore through the clearing. She looked half ready to murder someone, wings flaring sharp enough to cut moonlight. "I can't leave you alone for *five minutes* without you trying to burn the realm down! You can't do *anything* with witches. You know this!"

Jo froze. Her grip loosened, voice caught between guilt and fury. "It's not… what it…"

Lena's wings snapped open like knives. "You were *kissing* her! Witch, you may not know this, but fae and witches must never mix. It could be catastrophic for everyone!"

For one heartbeat, Jo looked at me, like she *dared* to make it worse.

So, naturally, I smiled. Sly. Wicked. "Yeah, and what of it? We sure did. What are you going to do about it?"

Jo's head whipped toward me. "What?!"

Ciaran nearly fell off his rock, cackling. "Gods, *finally!* I thought you two would never get there."

Of course, Ciaran played along, but Zane and Kael too?

"Who could've seen that coming?" Zane muttered, deadpan.

Kael smirked behind his mask. "Pity we didn't get to see it."

Jo sputtered, scarlet. "We didn't...I didn't...no..."

195

I leaned in harder, voice dripping honey.

"Sure, honey. Keep telling yourself that. Why erase the love we share, babe?"

Her grip tightened again.
Lena's eyes went murder-bright.

"This isn't a joke, *Morgan!*" she snapped. "Do you want the Court to make a spectacle of you? They already think you reek of her. They'll kill you, and I can't protect you this time."

I should've stopped.

I didn't.

"How did you protect me, Lena?" I shot back. "You let them drag me away. What's one kiss? They already think we rutted. You didn't help with that."

Jo looked like she might drop dead on the spot.
And gods, I wanted to laugh.

Joanna

Oh. My. *Gods.*

Morgan actually said we kissed and *kept it going.*

We didn't.
I mean, I wanted to, but still.

My stomach flipped, my brain short-circuited,
my entire existence collapsed into *what is
happening.*

I wanted to scream, or hex her, or crawl into a
hole and die.

And then Morgan, wicked as ever, bit her lip and added, "In my defense, Lena, she's better at kissing than you."

I almost died.

Then I started *wheeze-laughing.*

"Oh, is that so, Morgan?" I gasped. "Didn't know we could add a third to the party!"

Ciaran and Zane *high-fived.*
"SCORE!"

Morgan just blinked, like she couldn't believe I'd said it.

Lena, however, didn't laugh.
"DON'T you realize the danger you're putting us in?"

The tension cracked somewhere between fury and hilarity, and before I knew it, we were marching into the woods like idiots.

Lena stomped in front, all righteous fury and authority. Behind her, the rest of us trailed, combusting from laughter.

Ciaran hummed. Kael glided like a smug ghost. Zane smirked for once.

Morgan brushed my shoulder, just enough to make my ribs flutter, and grinned.

"Why are you grinning?" I hissed.

"Because Lena looks like she wants to murder us. I think it'd be funny to kiss you for real."

I almost tripped. "Morgan! She'll *hear!* And do you ever shut up?"

"Nope," she said. "Nice to be listened to for once."

She leaned close, whispering like a bad narrator from a nature show.

"Observe...the mighty *Grumpus.* Note her aggression. Her stomps. Her majestic glare..."

Ciaran snorted. "Gods, she *is*! What's next, a minotaur with a bad hair day?"

Morgan crouched, claw-hands out, and let out a shriek like a dying mule.
"Rrrreeehhh!"

I *wheezed.* Ciaran bent double. "Again!"

Zane groaned. "Strike me down. I've fallen into Lucifer's trap."

"Don't tempt me," Lena snapped.

Morgan stomped in circles like a deranged goat.

"Fear meeee! I am the terror in these woods!"

"You sound like a goat being sat on."

"I'm majestic."

"You're a menace."

"Majestic Menace!" Ciaran declared, holding up a stick like a scepter.

Even Kael huffed. "Accurate."

Morgan bellowed a ballad at the top of her lungs: "OH YE UNFAIR TRESPASSERS LIE, WHAT WILL WE DO, OR MUST WE DIE!"

I slid down a tree, choking on spit. "Stop! You're *atrocious!*"

Ciaran fell face-first into the dirt. "No, keep going!"

Morgan howled another verse. "OH, VALIANT BABES OF NIM, LORDS AND LADIES HAVE THY WHIM!"

That did it, Zane *actually laughed.*
Kael grabbed his tunic, *howling.*

Ciaran pointed. *"History!* They laughed! Write this down!"

My ribs hurt. My lungs burned.
I side-eyed Morgan, who gave me a look as delicate as sin.

"What?" she asked, all false innocence. "You want another kiss, babe?"

Ciaran tripped again. "Divine comedy. I can die in peace!"

"A kiss?" I mocked. "At least I don't get hot and bothered over floor décor."

The woods froze.

Morgan's head snapped toward me. "You did *not.*"

"Oh, I did," I said sweetly. "Rug Daddy misses you."

Morgan went pale.

"Wait, Rug Daddy?" Ciaran perked up.

Zane blinked. "What?"

Kael tilted his head. "Yes. Explain."

Morgan covered her face. "It was *one time.* The rug had a good weave, okay?"

I wheezed so hard I saw stars. "Yeah, you said thank you afterward."

Ciaran screamed, "THANK YOU!" and rolled into a bush.

"Tragic," Zane muttered.

Morgan threw her arms up. "I was being polite!"

"You curtsied."

"It was a reflex!"

We all lost it.

Even Kael looked like he might actually die of laughter.

Lena spun mid-step, jaw tight. "If the Court finds us, we'll be in danger."

Morgan wiped tears from her cheeks, grin wicked. "Yeah—squirrel danger."

"Rug danger," I added.

Ciaran collapsed again.

Kael muttered, "Danger from Morgan's singing."

"Can confirm," Zane said.

Morgan tried to defend herself. "It was a *fine tune!*"

"If you squint, hold your breath, and pass out, it might sound like a song," I sputtered.

Lena's jaw locked like stone. "This isn't a joke. They're coming. And when they find you tangled up with her..." She stopped herself, voice cracking. "Don't expect me to save you."

The laughter died in my chest. The fire in her words chilled the air.

Morgan didn't say anything.
For once, silence.

And all I could think was that maybe Lena wasn't warning us out of duty.

Maybe she was warning us because she'd already lost too much.

CHAPTER 20
The Grumpus Ascends
Morgan

Lena vanished into the trees like a bat out of hell, wings flared, hair wild, muttering curses that probably translated to *"I'm going to murder them with a tree branch and feel nothing."*

Behind her, the five of us trailed like a parade no one asked for.

Jo raised both hands solemnly. "She has ascended to the realm of pissed-off forest aunties."
I put a hand over my heart. "May she find peace and a better attitude."

207

"Peace denied," Ciaran declared. "But oh gods, she's glorious when she's furious."

Zane's side-eye could've split bark. "You're insufferable."

"And yet, beautiful," Ciaran said, executing a bow that belonged in an opera house, not a swamp.

Kael's mask tilted a fraction. "Incorrect."

I snorted. "He's not wrong though. You've got gremlin energy, Ci."

"Finally, recognition," Ciaran beamed, tossing his hair like a deranged pageant queen.

We walked a few beats in mock silence before I cupped my hands around my mouth and shouted into the woods:

"WE'LL BEHAVE IN TEN TO TWELVE BUSINESS YEARS!"

Jo clapped. "That's generous."

"I thought so."

"Generous?" Zane muttered. "That's a death sentence."

Kael's shadows flickered lazily at his boots. "Optimistic."

Ciaran gasped theatrically. "Wait. Did *Deer Prince* and *Shadow Boy* just agree with me? Someone carve this into stone!"

"Shut up," Zane said flatly.

We meandered more than marched, the forest sighing around us like it knew better than to get involved.

Jo looped her arm through mine, all mock sweetness. "You realize we're probably going to die tragically, right?"

"I've accepted that," I said. "But I'll look fabulous doing it."

"You have moss in your hair."

"Bold of you to assume it isn't a fae fashion statement."

"Bold of you to assume I won't start calling you *Moss Goblin*."

"I accept my title with honor. First of my name. Chaos-born. Squirrel-feared."

Ciaran howled. "YES! Moss Goblin, Slayer of Squirrels, Curtsier of Rugs!"

Jo nearly tripped from laughing. "Careful, the forest is full of betrayal."

"You're full of something," I shot back.

"Charm?"

"Gremlin energy."

"Same thing, really."

Kael's voice slid through the air, calm as always.

"Gremlin suits you."

Jo smirked. "See? Even he agrees."

We reached a clearing where light spilled through the canopy like melted gold. The air was thick with the smell of pine and damp earth; the moss underfoot hummed faint, like it remembered songs older than us.

Jo spun in a slow circle, eyes bright. "Okay, but this part? This part's pretty."

"You're pretty," I blurted before my brain could stop my mouth.

Her head snapped toward me. For once, no-comeback. Just that soft, dangerous smirk. "Smooth."

"Oh, gods above," Ciaran groaned, dragging his hands down his face. "*JUST KISS ALREADY!* I can't keep watching this foreplay banter."

Zane folded his arms. "Spare us."

Jo groaned into her hands. "You three are the worst."

Kael tilted his head slightly. "Correct."

"And yet," Ciaran said, grinning wide, "we're your audience."

Joanna

Morgan was pacing the edge of the clearing now, wings twitching with exaggerated drama.

"I'm practicing for when Lena comes back and yells at us again," she announced. "I need distraction tactics."

"So, your plan is flirt until she forgets you're unbearable?" I asked.

"Yes," Morgan said solemnly. "Or until she flies into a tree mid-rant. Either works."

Ciaran slapped his thigh. "Gods, if that happens, I'm writing *The Rant and the Tree*. Instant classic."

"Wouldn't rhyme," Zane said flatly.

"Doesn't have to," Ciaran shot back. "It's art."

Kael's shadows stirred, curling like smoke around his boots. "Tragedy is the truest art."

Ciaran pointed. "See? Mask boy gets it."

I shook my head, trying not to smile. "You're all idiots."

Morgan grinned. "You say that like it's new."

We lingered there in the clearing, throwing jokes like knives, pretending the world wasn't hunting us. For a while, laughter filled the air, bouncing off bark and stone.

Morgan was mid-rant about the squirrel's supposed spy network,

"Rodents, pigeons, probably deer too. They're unionized, Jo."

I opened my mouth to fire back,
when it happened.

The **wind changed.**

Not much. Just enough. The kind of shift that
sneaks in sideways, barely there until your skin
prickles and your gut tightens like it knows
something you don't.

I stopped laughing.

Morgan did too. Mid-sentence. Mouth half-open.
Eyes narrowing.

"Did it just get colder," I whispered, "or did you
just fart?"

"Yeah," she said slowly.

"To which one?"

"Both." Her stare stayed wide, unblinking.
Ciaran froze halfway through a laugh. "...Okay, I
hate that answer."

The trees felt closer now. Not visibly, just *felt*. Like they'd leaned in when we stopped paying attention.

The gold light thinned into gray. Shadows bled long. The air grew heavy, thick as wet cloth. Even the forest seemed to hush.

Something was here.

Something watching.

And suddenly, every joke we'd thrown into the air felt like a prayer that had gone unanswered.

Chapter 21
Fire and Shadow
Morgan

The fire hissed sideways, like something exhaled from the wrong direction.

A chill rolled through the clearing, sharp enough to raise the hairs on my neck.
And then I saw her.

Smoke shaped like a woman shimmered at the tree line; tall, elegant, wrong. Her form shifted in and out of the air, half-light, half-shadow. Horns curled sleek from her temples, catching the dim firelight like polished bone. Her grin stretched too wide, too knowing.

She didn't move.

Just breathed in.

Slow. Deliberate. Like she was *tasting* us.

A succubus.

Fantastic. The kind that fed on emotion, fear, rage, lust. Basically, our entire group love language.

The tether under my ribs snapped hot. Every nerve screamed danger.
Before my mind caught up, my body moved, pure instinct.

I lunged and wrapped Jo in my wings, cocooning her against me.

She stiffened, gasped, her breath ghosting against my chest. "What are you doing, Morgan?"

"Shh." I tightened my hold. "There's something out there."

Anxiety crawled under my skin. My fingers twitched. And before I could stop myself, I realized what I'd done.

The little *wooden horse* was in my hand. The one from her cabin.

Jo's gaze snapped to it. Her witchmark flared to life, burning blue through the fabric of her sleeve.

"That…*THAT WAS IN MY CABIN!*"

I flinched at the word *my*, curling my fist around it like it might bite me. "It's just a toy! I was curious! I wanted to know what it meant to you."

Her voice broke sharp, cracking through the night.

"You had no right. You tied me up, left me like a dog, and now you're holding my mother's gift like it belongs to you!"

The tether slammed between us, burning, relentless. My throat went dry, rage flaring to match hers. I wanted to drop the horse. Gods, I wanted to. But the heat surged through me, fury fueling every vein.

"I WAS DOING MY JOB!" I shouted. "AT LEAST I DIDN'T FOLLOW THROUGH AND KILL YOU!"

Joanna

"NO!"
My voice tore through the clearing, hoarse and wild. "You *chose* that! You chose to steal, to lie—to *leave me there!*"

The fury came out of me like fire. I shoved her. Hard. Pure reflex.

She shoved back.

We shoved again.
And again.

Back and forth, chest to chest, wings flaring, hair snapping in the wind. Sparks cracked between us, literal sparks, blue and gold, where our hands collided.

The heat under my skin roared alive, my Witchmark blazing through the fabric, pulsing in time with my heartbeat.

"Morgan, stop…" I tried, but the words vanished in the fire roaring in my veins.

The succubus grinned wider. She leaned closer, feeding on every heartbeat, every scream. Her eyes were black, pupils dilated wide as void. She was *drinking us in.*

Every shout.

Every shove.

Every shred of anger made her stronger.

I couldn't stop. My hands burned where they met hers. My vision swam. My breath hitched.

I grabbed her arms. She grabbed mine. Heat exploded between us.

And then—
heaviness.
Crushing.

My eyelids dragged low. The fire blurred. The succubus laughed, soft and delighted, as the world tilted sideways.

Morgan

The tether thrummed once—then snapped taut
like a whip.

My body went weightless.
Then heavy.
Too heavy.

Exhaustion slammed me, thick and sudden. My
knees buckled—and hers did too.

We collapsed together, tangled in wings and arms,
falling into the moss. Her hair brushed my cheek,
soft and damp. Our heartbeats slowed in sync.

Slower.

Slow.

Still.

The firelight flickered once, twice—then
dimmed.

Through the haze, I saw her.
The succubus.

Still smiling.
Satisfied.
And then, she vanished like smoke.

Ciaran

I blinked.

One second they were screaming bloody murder, ready to claw each other's eyes out.

The next, silence.

Then, *collapse.*

Jo in Morgan's arms. Morgan's wings wrapped around her like some tragic painting. Both out cold on the moss.

I rubbed my eyes. "What the hell just happened?"

Zane's jaw locked. "I don't know."

Kael tilted his mask, shadows writhing uneasily at his feet. "Strange."

I tried to laugh, but it came out thin.

"Weirdest lovers' spat I've ever seen. None of mine ended in synchronized napping."

Zane shot me a glare sharp enough to peel bark.

"This isn't a joke, Ciaran."

"Everything's a joke until someone dies," I said softly. But the chill crawling down my spine didn't feel like humor.

Kael stepped forward, studying them.

"They're alive. Bound by something stronger than sleep."

Zane crouched beside them, gaze flicking at the burned grass beneath their hands. The scorch marks curved like runes, spirals of blue and gold.

"The tether reacted," he muttered. "And something...fed on it."

Ciaran swallowed hard. "Fed? Like—fed *fed?*"

Kael's voice was barely a whisper. "Yes."

The fire guttered low, cinders sighing into ash.

For a long, terrible moment, none of us spoke.

And somewhere in the distance, between the trees...

something laughed.

CHAPTER 21
Three idiots one brain cell
Ciaran

Morgan and Jo had fallen asleep out of nowhere, tangled together like vines.

This wouldn't have been so weird if they hadn't been spitting venom at each other *seconds* before. One minute: screaming, threatening, murder-eyes. The next: cozy lovers in some tragic fae opera, her wing draped like a blanket and everything.

It was either magic or insanity. Both seemed plausible.

"Oh well," I muttered, rubbing my hands. "If you can't beat the chaos, drink through it."

Because really, what else do you do when the two most emotionally unstable people in your group faint mid-argument and start spooning like fate itself shipped them?

"To us!" I shouted, raising my cup to the heavens. "Have a drink, you fools! They're asleep anyway, no need to waste this beautiful, possibly cursed night!"

Zane hesitated half a heartbeat before joining me.

Kael just stared at his drink like he was reading prophecy in the foam, then shrugged and drank too.

And just like that, the three of us were blubbering fools.

We were supposed to be *making a fire.*

Instead, we were drinking and laughing like idiots lost in the woods.

Which explains why Zane, mighty Antler Boy himself, dragged over a log the size of a baby elk and tried to set it ablaze just by glaring at it.

"KiNdaLeeng…" he slurred.

What he meant was *kindling.*

I grinned so wide my face hurt. "That's not kindling, that's a forest, you delicate deer prince. You're rebuilding the habitat, not lighting it!"

Kael swayed nearby like a haunted scarecrow, shadows dancing lazily around him. He poked the dirt with a stick, muttering to himself like he was negotiating rent with the underworld. His mask gleamed faintly in the firelight, the shadows shifting like they were laughing too.
This night was going to be *great.*

Zane

Ciaran was half-useless because he couldn't stop laughing.

He hadn't lifted a finger, just heckled me while swaying like a happy drunk bard.

"It would be useful if you actually helped instead of mocking me," I growled, jabbing at the log again. Sparks sputtered, died.

"I *am* helping," he said solemnly, raising his cup like a priest at communion. "Moral support and valuable comedy."

Kael suddenly waved both arms over the pile like a deranged prophet. "Rise!" he whispered. His ale tilted, half of it spilling into the moss.

"Party foul!" Ciaran screamed, clutching his chest like someone had died.
I rubbed my temple. We were doomed if anything actually attacked us tonight.

Kael

The shadows danced with us. They liked the chaos.

They *always* like the chaos.

"Air," I declared, sprawled on my back now, pointing at the sky. "The fire needs… air."

Ciaran leaned down and blew so hard he nearly face-planted into the log. Smoke puffed straight into his face. He hacked like a goose dying in a pond.

Zane actually *snorted.*

I laughed too, quietly, but still. The sound felt strange. Foreign. Almost… nice.

Ciaran

Finally, *smoke.* Pathetic, weak, curling—but smoke, nonetheless.

I staggered back, arms spread wide.

"BEHOLD! The Antlered Prince and the Hollow Corpse have summoned FIRE! Oh, ye gods of incompetence, bless this miracle!"

The smoke fizzled.

"Don't jinx it, Ciaran!" Zane barked, stabbing at the pile like he could intimidate it into ignition. Kael hummed ominously, still half-sprawled.

I nearly peed myself laughing. Funniest night of my life.

Zane

Then it happened. The spark caught. Tiny, but real.
Flame.
I exhaled for what felt like the first time in an hour.
Ciaran clapped like he'd witnessed divine birth. "OH, THANK ALL GODS. THREE IDIOTS, ONE BRAIN CELL, AND A LOT OF ALCOHOL—AND WE DID IT!"

He collapsed backward into the moss, legs in the air, wheezing with joy.

Kael whispered from the ground, voice reverent, "The fire... it lives."

Ciaran

I jumped to my feet. "Huzzah! A song! A dance! A night of romance! Three wasted cavemen made fire!"

I stomped in a circle, ale sloshing everywhere. "Oh, witch of curls, oh fae of wings, snore me the song true love sings!"

Zane sat sharpening his knife like a grumpy statue. Unacceptable.

"Come, Antler Boy!" I lunged, grabbing his wrist. He hesitated maybe two seconds. "Please no." "Yes, deer boy!"

And then we were spinning in circles like idiots. Boots kicking sparks, shadows leaping high, the forest echoing with laughter.

Halfway through the dance, Zane went pale.

Zane

The world tilted.

Ciaran spun me again. Firelight blurred. My stomach lurched.

"Stop," I gritted, swallowing bile.
He spun faster.

I shoved him away, doubled over, hands on my knees.

Gods. I was going to heave.

Ciaran collapsed in hysterics, tears streaming. "THE DELICATE DEER PRINCE CAN'T HANDLE A LITTLE SPINNING!"

I spat into the dirt. "You're too loud. You'll wake them."

Kael

I clapped. Once. Slowly.
"Good," I said.

Ciaran howled louder. Zane groaned into his sleeve.

The shadows leaned closer, curious.

Ciaran

Then I saw them.

Across the fire, the witch and the fae shifted closer in their sleep. Morgan's wing drooped protectively over Jo. Jo's curls brushed Morgan's jaw.

And then came the snoring.

Not delicate snores. No.

Jo *whistled* like a kettle about to explode. Morgan *rumbled* like a bear dying dramatically. Together, they sounded like a haunted flute duet played underwater.

I nearly spat my drink across the fire. "LISTEN TO THAT. Gods above, it's *art!*"
Zane muttered, "They're tired."

"They're *in love*," I countered, clutching my heart.

"Hear it! That's the song of passion!"

Kael nodded gravely. "Yes. They breathe like dying animals. This means affection."

I wept. "Poetic bastards."

Zane

Their noses brushed. Just barely.

Ciaran seized my arm and eyes huge. "DID YOU SEE THAT? THEY'RE GOING TO KISS!"

"They're *breathing*," I muttered.

"BREATHING LOOKS LIKE PRE-KISS FOREPLAY TO ME!" he hissed.

Kael's eyes gleamed faintly. "Air pulls them together."

I wanted to strangle both of them.

Ciaran

I slammed my cup down. "BETS! Who's in? I'll give my boots if they kiss before dawn!"

Kael raised his cup solemnly. "I'll give you this cup."

"I accept!" I howled. "What about you, Zaney boy?"

Zane muttered, "By the gods, you actually said my name." Which wasn't a no.

I grinned. "If they actually kiss, I'll officiate the wedding right here. We've got fire, witnesses, alcohol, what more do you need?"

Kael

The flames popped, sparks leaping high.
Their lips almost touched. Almost.

Ciaran screamed into his fist, kicking the air like he'd been stabbed.

Zane groaned, dragging his hands down his face.
"They will," I murmured. "But not tonight."

236

Ciaran collapsed into the moss. "TRAGEDY. CURSED BY THE GODS. ART DENIED."

The shadows laughed with me.

Ciaran

And that was our night:

Drunk.

Freezing.

Mocking each other under the stars.

We roasted each other worse than the boar.

We argued about destiny and squirrels and who would die first in a horror story.

And somewhere between the laughter and the ash, we all stopped feeling quite so cursed.

They didn't kiss. Of course they didn't.
But gods, it was the best entertainment I've had in years.

CHAPTER 22

Antlers, shadows, and bullshit
Ciaran

By the time the fire caught and Zane finished being sick, the worst of our chaos was wrung out of us.

The laughter burned itself out. The ale was half-gone. Smoke curled low and bitter on the tongue, weaving through the cold like a ghost too stubborn to leave.

The forest had gone quiet in that way that makes you think the world's listening.

Only the insects sang now, grinding, rasping, endless.

The dark pressed close, thick as breath. The kind of dark where you swear you see things move, and dark enough you almost believe them. The bottle passed slower between us. The jokes sagged under their own weight.

Even I started to feel that slow seep of truth that crawls in when you run out of laughter to block it. Across the fire, the witch and the fae were a tangle of limbs and bad decisions.

Slumped together like penguins in a blizzard of regret.

I barked a laugh anyway, because if I didn't, I'd start thinking about my wife, and that's a disaster for everyone.

"Gods above, would you *look* at them," I said, tossing a stick into the flames. Sparks hissed, and Morgan snored, actually *purred*. "If I didn't know better, I'd think those two actually liked each other."

Zane grunted from where he was hunched, poking the dirt like it had insulted him. Kael didn't move at all, still as carved bone, mask glinting in the firelight.

"Don't glare at me, boys," I added, smirking. "I'm not the one cuddling a witch. And you both know you want to see some action."

Kael's voice cut through flat and cold. "Please stop while you're ahead."

"Why would I?" I said, showing teeth. "The night's still young. The ale's still flowing. And I'm clearly the entertainment."

Their only answer was a pair of groans.

"Fine," I sighed, spreading my arms. "It's either laugh at these two or start crying. And we all know I'm prettier when I laugh."

Still nothing. Gods, they were hopeless.

Ciaran

"You know how I learned to hold a blade?" I asked finally, grinning like I was about to tell a joke.

Neither looked up.

Perfect.

"When I was ten, the Court tossed me into the pit with three older boys. Blindfolded. Said, *earn your way out.*"

I twirled the bottle, watching the firelight ripple across the glass. "I came out with a broken arm, a bloodied nose, and an eye so swollen I couldn't see out of it for a week. Guess who got praised?"

No one answered.

241

"Not me," I said, grin sharpening. "Guess what I learned? If I draw faster next time, maybe I'll bleed less."

The laugh that tore out of me was too loud, too sharp, the kind that sounds like it belongs to someone else.

Kael tilted his mask toward me. "That's really dark, Ciaran. Have you sought counsel?"

I wiped my eyes with my sleeve and laughed harder. "Look who's talking. You're made of gloom and cryptic nonsense. You *are* counsel."

Zane's jaw flexed, silent.

"Well?" I said, leaning in. "Hollow Boy admits to trauma. I admit I'm Court property. You, Antler Boy, what's your bedtime horror?"

Zane
I didn't look up.

I never do when they ask.

I just rubbed my thumb along the grooves in the iron bands strapped to my antlers. The metal was cold, smooth in places, but I could still feel where the runes were burned in, ridges of pain, sealed long ago. The firelight made them gleam like blood gone to rust.

"The herd says the bands make me strong," I said finally. My voice came out low, almost swallowed by the crackle of fire. "Restraint. Loyalty. Silence."

I huffed something that might've been a laugh. "Every time they press blood into the grooves, they tell me it's to make me stronger. But every time they do it…" I swallowed. "…I wonder if they're giving me strength, or chains."

The air felt heavier after that. I didn't like how quiet it got.
My hand dropped from the bands, but the ache stayed.

"At least it wasn't the knife," I muttered.
I felt them both look at me, but I didn't return it.
My eyes flicked, for half a second, toward Morgan.

243

She shifted in her sleep, wings twitching.
I looked away fast. Too fast.
The truth hung there anyway.

Ciaran

"There it is," I said, breaking the silence. "The broody deer prince *does* have feelings. I thought that scowl was just for decoration."

Kael's shadow stirred, the edges of it flickering like smoke caught in wind.

His voice came quiet, like he was telling himself. "An older boy taught me shadows. Held me down even when I didn't want to learn."

The firelight caught his mask as his fingers twitched. "He rots in the ground now. Not enough."

The air froze.

"My family left me in the Hollow," he added softly. "Easier to forget the shadow-marked than feed them."

The silence stretched until it hurt.

I laughed, because I didn't know what else to do. "Gods, that's grim. Alright, fine, if we're sharing trauma, who's got another round?"

Zane shifted beside me. His voice was rougher this time. "Never good enough for my brothers. No matter how hard I fought, how much I bled, it was always, 'again.' Or worse, 'unworthy.'"

I whistled low. "Family," I said. "The curse that keeps giving."

The branches above us tangled black against the stars. "Nothing like family to make sure you never feel enough."

Kael's voice slipped through the quiet. "Or not having one at all."

That one hit different.

Ciaran

I sprawled on the moss, staring up at the branches.

"Gods, you two are terrible at bedtime stories. Dead mentors, antler chains, childhood trauma, it's a wonder we haven't been recruited as the Court's official depression squad."

Neither smiled

.

"Fine," I said, quieter now, watching the fire shrink to embers. "I'll keep the jokes. Because if I didn't laugh…" I trailed off. "I don't think I'd want to live."

The fire popped, like it understood.

And for half a heartbeat, both of them nodded.

Kael's shadows coiled closer, curling around him like a blanket. His breathing slowed.
I let my grin fade as sleep dragged me down.

Zane

I stayed awake.
Couldn't help it.

246

The forest never really sleeps, just waits. Every creak of the trees sounded like breath. Every flicker of the fire painted faces that weren't there. The others drifted off, their laughter gone to ghosts.

Ciaran muttered once in his sleep, something about rugs and squirrels. Kael didn't move, though his shadow still twitched like it dreamed without him.
I stared into the woods, the edges of the dark moving wrong. The night air bit cold against my skin, but the bands around my antlers pulsed warm, too warm.

I brushed them again, whispering the old herd prayer. "Run silent. Strike true. Return as one." But the woods whispered something else back.

Not words. Just breath.

A slow exhale that didn't belong to any of us. My hand froze midair.

Something was out there. And it was watching.

CHAPTER 23

The First Panic

Joanna

Morning dew clung cool against my skin, trailing goose pimples down my arm. The air was damp and sharp in my lungs, every breath tasting of wet moss and ash.

Pale light threaded through my lashes; beads of water clung there and gleamed silver.
For one fragile moment, the world seemed peaceful.

Then I shifted —

And I felt **weight that wasn't mine.**

I froze.

An arm curved around my waist. Legs tangled with mine, too soft, too careful to be any of the boys.

Feathers draped over us like a blanket, curving me in, cocooning me against the chill.

My cheek rested against someone's shoulder. My heartbeat pounded loud in my ear.

Thump. Thump. Thump.

Who am I sleeping next to?

I turned my head and saw **Morgan.**

Panic jolted through me, fast and electric. The last thing I remembered was being furious, her shouting, my magic flaring, wings snapping open like a storm.

And now, here we were.

Wrapped together like something painted for a chapel ceiling.

The air reeked faintly of ale.

Oh no.

Did we...?

In front of the boys?

Gods help me.

What the hell happened last night?

Morgan stirred. Her lashes flickered, breath warm against my collarbone. She caught my panic instantly.
The words spilled out of me before I could stop them.
"Did we...?"

Her voice rasped low, a velvet scrape against the quiet.
"Did we… eat a boar? Yes. It was tasty."
She blinked at me, sly. "But something tells me that's not what you meant. Did we… give in to temptation?"

My stomach dropped.

"I…I don't know," I stammered.

Her grin curved slow and dangerous. "Did we… fool around?"

"Morgan…" I whined, trying to hide my face.
"Did we cross that line? Did we sneak a peek? Did we…"

"Please stop talking." My palms covered my face, heat burning up my neck.

She leaned in, voice a purr.

"Did we explore the caverns? Shake the sheets? Grope for trout in a peculiar river? Did we…" her mouth brushed dangerously close, "come together?"

"GODS!" I snapped, mortified. "Shut up!"

Morgan only grinned wider.

"Or did we just... sleep together?"

"MORGAN!"

I nearly woke the whole camp.

Zane

"No," I said flatly, not looking up from my blade. "You just fell asleep on one another."

Both their heads whipped toward me like they'd been struck.

"WHAT?!" they said in perfect, outraged harmony.

"You collapsed together," I clarified, dragging the whetstone once more across steel.

252

"It wasn't that exciting. You used each other for warmth."

A pause. Then, deliberately: "Very riveting." Silence.

Then Ciaran snorted somewhere behind me, muttering, "Best romance I've ever not seen."

Joanna

"Well..." I huffed, still red. "You snore."

Morgan's smirk sharpened. "And you drool. We're even."

"I do not!"

"You do." She tapped her collarbone, where a faint damp patch glistened in the morning light.

Heat crawled up my throat. I blurted the first thing that came to mind.

"Well, I guess that drool's all mine."

Morgan

Mine.

She said it so easily. Like it meant nothing. Like it didn't scrape bone.

But the word hit me like a blade in the ribs— hard, direct, **too familiar.**

Ines's voice echoed inside me, slick with silk and cruelty:

You're mine.

Sudden, memory surged.

The scent of smoke.
The sound of iron.

Feathers wrenched from my back in white-hot agony.

Blood splattering on marble.

The shriek of metal cutting through flesh.

Her hand at my neck, forcing me down.
Her breath hot against my ear.

You belong to me.

The scream of the saw.
The weight of the cuffs.
The sound my wings made when they hit the
floor.

The brand came next pressed into raw skin where
my wings had been.

I can still smell it.
Still hear it hiss.
Still feel the heat crawling inside my bones.

The air left my lungs.
I couldn't breathe.
Not again. Not this.
The morning disappeared.

The fire, the laughter, Jo, gone.
All I could feel was the chain tightening again.

Joanna

At first, I thought she was ignoring me—thinking up another clever line. But she wasn't moving.

Her face had gone slack. Her eyes unfocused. Then the trembling started.
"Morgan?" My stomach plunged.
No answer.

I leaned in, shaking her shoulder. "Hey, Morgan. It was just a joke. Earth to fae girl, come on."

Nothing.

Her breaths came short and shallow, gasping through invisible panic.

Her whole body trembled, wings twitching like they remembered pain.

"MORGAN!" I shouted, voice cracking.
Nothing again.

I cupped her face in both hands. Her skin was cold and damp, her pulse wild beneath my thumbs. Tears prickled the corners of my eyes.

"ZANE!" I screamed, throat raw. "Zane, I need your help—something's wrong with her!"

Zane

Jo's scream split the morning like a blade.
I was already up, crossing the clearing in three strides.
     Morgan was crumpled on the moss, gasping, clawing at nothing.

Her chest rose too fast, too shallow. Her eyes were wide and wild, staring at something none of us could see.

I dropped to my knees beside her. "Morgan."
No response. Just shaking.

     Her feathers quivered like they were remembering being torn out. The scent of fear hit the air—raw, metallic, and old.

I'd seen soldiers like this before, men broken by the things they couldn't forget.

But this wasn't the battlefield.

This was worse.

Whatever was tearing through her wasn't happening *outside*.

It was carved **inside her.**

Something the Court had put there and never taken back.

I reached out, steady and slow, hand hovering over her shoulder but not touching.

Her whole body convulsed, breath hitching hard. "Breathe," I said softly, though I knew she couldn't hear me.

"Come on, Morgan. Breathe." The world felt like it was holding its breath with her.

CHAPTER 24
Grounded
Joanna

Zane was at my side in an instant.
I still had my hands cupped to Morgan's face, my
thumbs trembling against her temples.

Her chest was heaving like she was drowning
on dry land, breath tearing out of her lungs too
fast, too hard. Her eyes, gods, her eyes were wide
and glassy, reflecting a world I couldn't see.

"Come on," I whispered. "Breathe with me."

I exaggerated the motion, big inhale, loud exhale. "In and out... follow my rhythm."

But she didn't. Her breaths only came faster, harsher, like each one scraped her throat raw.

"Jo."

Zane's voice, low, calm, unshakable.

He crouched beside me, steady as stone. "Let me." I hesitated but shifted back, desperate because nothing I was doing was working.

He took over like he'd done before. His tone went even, clipped but soft. "Morgan, listen to me. Five things you can see."

No response. Just that empty, haunted stare. "Four things you can touch. The ground. Your cloak. My knife. Jo's sleeve."

At *knife*, her breath hitched, sharp. Then she shattered into frantic gasps.
Her hands clawed at her ribs like she could dig the fear out.

"Shit," Zane muttered under his breath. "She's not grounding. She's gone under."

I couldn't take it anymore. Watching her tear herself apart, something open in me.
Instinct slammed through before thought could catch up.

I moved.

I pressed my forehead to hers—skin to skin, no space, just heat and trembling and tears I didn't remember deciding to shed. My pulse hammered against her.

"Morgan." My voice came out low, steady, shaking anyway. "You're here. You're safe."
Her chest stuttered once, then again.

I said it again, louder this time, firmer. "You're safe. You're with me."

Her body trembled under my hands. Another breath. A jagged one. Then slower. Then slower still.

The tremor eased by inches. The storm broke apart into ragged, uneven exhales.
Finally, the sound of breath filled the space between us again.

Morgan
The world had been nothing but sound and pressure,

A scream with no air.

Knives in my lungs.

Hands I couldn't see holding me down.

Then, her.

Joanna's palms, hot against my skin. Her forehead pressed to mine. Her breath guiding me until it

262

didn't hurt to try.

Her voice, *I'm here. You're safe.*

The memory's grip loosened.
The brand still burned, but it was distant now.

And for the first time in forever, I felt
something like air slide back into my body.
Ugly. Gasping. Real.

A laugh cracked out of me, half sob, half sound.

"You're crying on me," I rasped. My throat hurt.

"And if you're going to get this close, we might as
well kiss."

Her eyes widened, bright, wet, furious. Color
rushed her cheeks.

"Gods, you're insufferable," she whispered, still
pressed against me.

"Accurate." I smiled, small and trembling. "So…
are you going to, or not?"

She grinned through her shaking. "You're
impossible."
"Also, accurate."

Ciaran

I groaned awake to the sound of heavy breathing
and dramatic tension.

Blinking through the dawn haze, I spotted it:
Joanna forehead-to-forehead with Morgan, Zane
crouched beside them like a knight mid-crisis.
Gods above.

"She's a whole adult," I muttered. "Why can't she
just deal with her emotions like the rest of us?"

Kael

The mask tilted. Shadows coiled faintly around his
shoulders.
"She may need professional help," he said flatly.

Zane

"ENOUGH."

My voice cracked like thunder. Both of them flinched.

"This isn't nerves," I said, each word cutting through the quiet. "It's not a bad mood. It's not

your everyday anxiety people joke about."
I pointed to where Morgan still shivered in Joanna's arms.

"What you're seeing, that's her body in revolt. She's not choosing this. She's trapped inside it." Ciaran's mouth opened for another smart remark. I didn't let him.

"You don't get it because you've never *been* there," I snapped. "This isn't a tantrum. Her body thinks she's dying."

The fire crackled low. No one spoke.

Kael's shadows curled tight around his boots. Ciaran looked away, his usual grin gone.

I lowered my voice, steady again. "So, you don't mock this. You don't stand there staring. You help. You anchor her until she finds her way back."

The silence that followed was thick, heavy, like the woods themselves were listening.

Joanna

I tightened my hold on Morgan, pressing our foreheads together again. The warmth of her breath steadied, syncing with mine.

Zane's words lingered, low and solid, wrapping the edges of the chaos like armor. Morgan's wings twitched once beneath my palms, weak but alive. Her breaths steadied, no longer fighting themselves.

She was finally here.

And so was I.

And for the first time since last night, I believed she might stay.

Chapter 25
Anchored and Bound
Joanna

I was still holding her.

My palms cupped Morgan's face, my forehead pressed to hers, refusing to let her drift. Her sweat clung to my hands, slick and salt-sharp. She trembled even through the scraps of humor she tried to force out, voice catching on half-laughs that weren't laughter at all.

Her arm hung weakly around my waist, more exhaustion than will. My legs were tangled with hers, our knees bruised against the moss. Her wings draped over us like a fallen tent, feathers brushing my throat with every shallow breath. Morgan's tunic had slipped halfway down her shoulder; our hair was a wreck, wild and matted with dew.

To an outsider, we'd look like lovers collapsed after a storm.
But I knew the truth.

I clung to her because if I let go, she'd shatter.

"Morgan..." My whisper trembled against her lips. "I'm here."

Her lashes fluttered once. A shiver ghosted through her. For one fragile heartbeat, it almost felt like peace, like the world might finally leave us alone.

Then the air snapped.

Chains of light erupted from nothing.
They struck like lightning, wrapping her wrists, her ankles, her throat. Morgan's body jerked hard,

yanked out from under me so violently that the ground itself seemed to lurch.
She hit the dirt with a scream. Feathers exploded around her in a white storm, scattering like torn wings.

"NO!" My voice ripped raw from my throat. "MORGAN!"

The forest bent. Shadows peeled apart like a curtain, and from them stepped the Court.

Their robes gleamed with cold light. The air stank of incense and iron.
Erelith led them.

His smile could have cut stone. "Well, well, well," he drawled, crouching low. He dragged one clawed finger down Morgan's cheek, slow enough to make her flinch. Blood welled, bright against her skin.

"Isn't this touching?"

Behind him, whispers slithered like snakes through grass:

"They must have mated right there."

"Already rolling in the dirt."

"They'll bring the realm down."

Rage split me open. They thought this was passion, *that* was what they saw? They didn't see the panic, the brokenness. They didn't see what they had done to her.

"LET HER GO!"

The words burst from me with my magic, feral and unbridled. Light tore free—bolts, waves, a storm so wild it cracked the air. Trees splintered. The ground buckled. My scream shook the clearing.
Erelith only laughed.
"You think you're a storm?" His teeth flashed.
"How cute. You're just a spark."
"I'LL KILL YOU!"

Another surge flared from me, a heat that scorched the dirt black and flung branches through the air. For one heartbeat, I thought I saw them stagger. I thought maybe—just maybe—I was enough.

Then I saw the boys kneel.

Kael. Zane. Ciaran.

Dropping like reeds in a storm.
The betrayal hit like a blade to the chest.
The Court moved as one.

Someone snapped their fingers.
The pain came.
It began in my chest, sharp, molten, then tore outward. Through bone, muscle, blood. It spread until every part of me burned.

I arched back, choking on a scream that clawed through my lungs. My body jerked, strings pulled by unseen hands.
The earth was cold under my back, but the fire in my veins devoured it. Dirt filled my mouth.

271

Sparks burst above me, violet, black, white, red, like stars dying.

My legs kicked. My hips jerked. My teeth clamped so hard I tasted blood. Nails scraped furrows into the ground, desperate for anything to hold.

Another scream ripped free—raw and inhuman.
"GAHHHHHHHHHHHHHHHHHHHH!"
And still the fire burned.

Kael

I didn't want to kneel.
But my body didn't ask.
The chains buried in my blood pulled tight, dragging me down before I could think. My forehead hit the dirt. The magic cut across my spine like knives.
Joanna's eyes met mine, wide, betrayed, and it gutted me.
She thought I'd chosen this. Gods, if she only knew.

I could hear her scream echo inside my ribs.
And I stayed bowed, because defiance meant
death.

Zane

The ground bit into my knees.
I stared at the soil because if I looked at her, I'd
break.

Jo's magic was still sparking in the air, burning
white-hot and wild—and she looked at us like we
were monsters.
Maybe we were.

Maybe we were cowards.

Maybe I was.

Her scream cut straight through my chest.
Every muscle screamed to move, to pull her up, to
stand between her and them.

But the Court's magic pressed me lower.
I'd spent my life being told to obey.
Now I was choking on the weight of it.

Ciaran

We folded like paper.
Maybe that's all we'd ever been.

Jo's scream cracked the air, pure fury, pure fear. It rattled something deep inside me, something that almost remembered bravery.

Almost.

The Court demanded obedience. We gave it.

Always.

Or died trying not to.

Morgan

I couldn't watch her anymore.

The sight of Joanna writhing in the dirt, every sound tearing through me, felt like my ribs might split.

I told myself this was just the tether, that the pain wasn't mine. But I knew better. It was.

It always was.

"STOP!"

The word ripped out of me, jagged and desperate. "Stop—please. I'll go with you. Just stop hurting her. I'll go."

The magic loosened. Joanna collapsed into the dirt, gasping, trembling.

Relief flooded me sharp enough to cut.

Kael and Zane grabbed me by the arms, their grips like iron. I didn't fight. What good would it do?

"Wait…" I twisted once toward her. "Let me just say this."

Her face was streaked with blood and ash. Her witchmark still flickered faintly, pulsing in time with her broken breaths.

"Joanna," I said, forcing the words out like poison, "we aren't friends. You were just a convenience. A warm body to keep me alive in the dark."

Every syllable burned my mouth.

She looked at me, horror, betrayal, heartbreak all at once, and it broke something in me I didn't know could still break.

Ciaran stayed bowed, shame dripping off him. Kael and Zane dragged me backward, toward the shadows, toward the waiting Court.
The world swallowed me whole.
And Joanna, broken, burned, and left behind again, crumpled in the dirt.

At least this time, I hadn't tied her up.

CHAPTER 26
Trial by Pain
Morgan

They didn't call it a trial.

Trials were meant for justice. For mercy. For a chance to speak, to beg, to prove yourself.

I didn't get any of that.

They just *assumed*.

Assumed what happened had happened, based on "evidence" that wasn't even there.

277

Assumed because it was easier. Because guilt is simpler when it already fits the story.

I wasn't given a chance.

This wasn't judgment.

It was *theater*.

Chains clanked when I shifted, iron biting into my wrists where they shackled me to the platform. My ankles locked wide, my knees forced apart like I was a carcass strung for display. My spine stretched taut, every breath grinding me against the post until I felt hollowed out.

Upright. Trapped.

The wood beneath my feet was slick. Rain. Or blood.
Probably both.
The crowd pressed in hungry, restless, ready for a show.
Not just the elders. *All* the factions came to watch.

The **Gilded** glittered in jewels, wine cups catching torchlight. Their laughter clinked louder than their gold. Among them, Erelith leaned back in his chair, smirking like the scene was his personal entertainment.

The **Dreadmarked** pounded weapons against stone, chanting like wolves scenting prey.
Ciaran lounged there, smirk painted cruel, while Lena beside him trembled, knuckles white, lips sealed around a scream she refused to let escape.

The **Antlered** hooted and drummed, bone charms rattling in rhythm.
Zane stood rigid among them—fists curled white, jaw locked, eyes fixed on the ground.

The **Hollowed** whispered behind masks, voices slicing the air like razors.
Kael tilted his head as though he could hear something no one else could.
And Ines—

Her stare cut straight through me, cold and knowing.
That look said it all: *I told you so.*

An elder stepped forward. His robes hung loose, parchment-thin. His eyes were stone. "You will be made an example."

The words struck harder than any lash could. The guards moved in. Fingers on my tunic. Ripping fabric. Cold air biting my bare skin. The whip unfurled in the elder's hand, seven tails, each one tipped with shards of glass, each knot threaded with spell-fire. The magic hissed like something alive.

I braced.

It fell.

The lash cracked the air.

Then split across my back.

A sound escaped me—half hiss, half animal. "Sssss—"

The crowd roared approval.

The lash rose again.
And again.
And again.

Leather. Fire. Flesh.

My screams clawed out of me raw and ragged.
They weren't even words anymore, just sound.
Something primal. Something that belonged to the
pain.

"Fae filth!"
"Whore!"
"Kill her!"

Their voices rose like thunder.

My wrists strained until the cuffs ran red. My
shoulders pulled so far back I thought they'd tear
from their sockets. Each strike blurred the world
into white light and sound.
"Please... please, no more..."

The words spilled out without permission. "I'll be
good, I'll stop, I didn't—please, stop!"

But mercy wasn't part of the script.
The lashes came faster. The fire hotter. Until all that came out of me were choked sobs, broken sounds.

Through the haze, I saw them.
Zane's hands shaking.
Kael whispering to something unseen.
Lena's tears balancing on the edge of her lashes.
And Ciaran,
Ciaran, whose smirk cracked just enough to show it wasn't real.
I didn't look at Ines.
I couldn't.

The whip stopped.

The air trembled. My body sagged against the chains, chest heaving, skin flayed in ribbons. Blood ran hot down my back and sides, pooling under my boots. I didn't dare turn. I didn't want to see what I'd become.

The elder set the whip aside.
And drew a dagger.

The sound of it scraping the sheath was worse
than the lash.
My body thrashed weakly, the iron cutting deeper.
"No, please…don't, please, I don't want to die…"

Steel touched my stomach.

Then dragged.
Slow.
From hip to hip.
White-hot agony.

My scream ripped through the chamber, tore
through the rafters, echoed off every wall.
"AHHHHHHHHHHHHHHHH! Please, gods, no!
PLEAAAAASE STOP, I CAN'T…"

The dagger lifted, slick with blood.
The crowd cheered.

Blood poured hot between my legs, down my
thighs, puddling at my feet. The platform gleamed
red under torchlight. The smell of iron and salt
and shame filled the air.

I wanted to vanish. To sink through the boards. To not exist where they could *see* me like this.
But the chains kept me upright.
Forced me to break in front of them.

"Help me," I gasped. To anyone. Everyone.
"Please... someone—"
No one moved.
Not even Lena, though her hands shook like she might.
I was alone.
The elder's voice sliced through my sobs, cold and final.
"Take her to the Gate."

Hands seized my arms. Iron clanked. The shackles tore loose, skin coming with them. I collapsed, but they didn't care.
They dragged me—across the stage, across my own blood. Each jolt split my wound wider. Each breath scraped my lungs raw.
"Please—don't send me there—please, gods, I'll do anything—"
The Gate loomed ahead.
Black. Vast. Waiting.

Its teeth of obsidian shimmered faint with runes
older than language. The air around it bent and
howled like a living thing.
They threw me forward.
Air ripped past my ears—cold, endless,
bottomless.
And then—
Dark.
A silence so deep it swallowed the sound of my
fall.

CHAPTER 27

The Hollow Gate

Morgan

I fell with the grace of a dropped anvil. Stone slammed my ribs so hard I felt something snap deep inside, a sound muffled by the wet crunch of impact. Air blasted out of my lungs and stayed gone; when I tried to yell, nothing came out but a dry rasp. For a jagged heartbeat, breathing was shards of glass.

When I finally dragged in air, it felt wrong, thick, distorted, almost *alive.*

They had thrown me into the Hollow Gate.

Where shadows breathe. Where souls rot. Where the Court sends things it doesn't want to kill clean.

Heat pressed in heavy and damp, stinking of decay, like living and dead things stewing together in a cauldron too long left on the fire. Every inhale coated my lungs with mildew and smoke until it felt like breathing mud.

The ground wasn't just stone. It pulsed. Black cracks split wide, weeping iron-stinking liquid. Glyphs crawled across the walls, angular, hooked, glowing faint blue like veins of trapped lightning. They pulsed brighter when I drew near, like the Gate itself was watching me.

Bone pillars arched inward, ribcages fused together, curving over me as though the chamber itself wanted to crush me into marrow.

I tried to push up, but pain tore through me. My arms trembled, refusing to hold my weight. Warmth slid from the dagger wound, sticky under my palm. Fingers shook against the floor.

And in my head, louder than a single word:

Convenient.

The word gutted me more than the blade had. How could I have thrown that at Joanna? Gods. If she were here, I'd tell her I didn't mean it. But I'd die here, and she would never know.

A growl rolled low through the chamber, vibrating the stone beneath me like a warning drum.

My head turned slowly. Something shifted in the glyph-light. My heartbeat stuttered.

The ground boomed.

A chimera stepped out.

Holy shit.

I was already torn open. I couldn't survive this.

It was carved from nightmares, lion's head, goat's body, serpent's tail; its limbs jointed wrong, claws screeching across stone. Ropes of saliva swung from its teeth, sizzling where they hit the floor. Its eyes glowed faint and cruel, catching the blue light like two coins from hell.

I dragged myself forward, nails tearing, blood smearing the floor in my wake. Every scrape split me wider. My breath rasped desperate.

I was going to die here.

My screams drowned beneath its growls, the echoes mocking me. The tail lashed, snapping the air. It wanted to play.

But I couldn't run.

My arms buckled. I collapsed.

The chimera lunged. Jaws clamped my leg. Its paw slammed inches from my skull, splintering stones, shards stinging my face. Shock rattled my bones. Its breath hit hot and sour, gagging me.

My hand closed on a jagged stone, my one chance.

I swung hard, smashing its head. Pain shot up my arm, but if I didn't fight, I'd be meat.

The beast staggered, bleeding. Then it collapsed with a ground-shaking boom.

The stone slipped from my fingers. My chest rose shallow and uneven. I stared at the carcass to be sure it was still, then let my head fall back. Blood pooled beneath me, seeping under my wings.

My vision dimmed.

I had won, barely.

The dark reached for me, and this time, I almost let it.

Joanna

She had said it, *convenient,* and it echoed like a blade turning inside me.

The tether yanked hard.

A tremor ran through me. The pull flickered, my stomach rolled, my skin went clammy. Even furious at her, I couldn't stand the thought of anything happening to her. Because I felt something I couldn't name.

"I should have followed her," I whispered.

The tether snapped.

Silence crashed in, louder than thunder. My knees hit the earth. I clawed at the dirt as tears blurred my sight. My heart hammered, frantic.

And then I was running.

I didn't know where, only that I had to find her.

Branches whipped my arms. Roots caught my feet. I didn't stop. The pull was faint but still there. If she was alive, I'd tear the forest apart to reach her. Because she was Morgan. And I couldn't lose her.

The air grew heavier the deeper I went, thick and cloying. Shadows gathered like fog.

And then—

A woman stepped out.

Her smile was too kind. Too smooth. A curve of lips that didn't belong in this place.

Her dress whispered like dead leaves when she moved. Her eyes caught the dim light like glass.

Half of me wanted to run.

The other half,
The other half wanted to stay.

CHAPTER 28
Ash and Hollow
Joanna

She stepped from the shadows with poise and ease,
too calm for the hour, too graceful for the woods.
Something in me whispered *she wasn't a friend,*
but out here, I didn't have many.

"You look like you need help," she said, voice
smooth as smoke. "Trying to find something? Or
someone?"

She lingered, smiling soft and dangerous all at
once.

"I know these woods. I can help. I promise."
Her words slid over me like shadows laid across stone,
soft, but unyielding.
I didn't know who she was.
But somehow, I had to trust her.
Because the forest was too quiet,
and her voice was the only sound that didn't feel like teeth.
So, I followed.
Why not follow the dainty stranger with the poise of a queen?
She *seemed* nice enough.
"My name is Ines," she purred.
"And yours?"
"Jolene," I lied.
"Ah… Jo." She tasted the name like poison.
"You don't strike me as someone who belongs here, 'Jolene.'"

We walked for what felt like hours,
the woods decaying around us—roots gnawed gray by time.
The tether in my ribs throbbed, aching with each step.
Morgan. Poor Morgan. I need to find you.

The trees grew darker, shapes bending like bones under moonlight.

The dim moon hung low and swollen when the Gate appeared,

a monolith of black stone veined with spiraling glyphs.

Whispers leaked from the cracks between worlds.

Help me...

Don't come in...

I hesitated.

Ines didn't.

"We should keep moving," she said, voice lilting like a lullaby.

"You're running out of time."

"Time?" My jaw locked. "I never said I was in a hurry."

"Oh, don't worry, kitten," she smiled, eyes gone bright and cruel.

"You'll find your precious Morgan."

Ice crawled up my spine.

"I never said who I was looking for—"

I spun.

She was already staring at me with something that wasn't kindness.

Hatred. Hunger.

Her hands slammed into my back.

The world tore open.

Darkness folded over me, cold, endless, absolute.
And I was swallowed whole.

Zane

We'd followed Ines from the start.
Ghosts among the trunks.

The fog hung thick as old rot, every breath
tasting like mold and memory.
I knew what she was doing. Knew how this would
end.

And when I saw her find Joanna, my gut
turned to stone.
This couldn't end well.

Joanna followed her like a lost pup.
Every nerve in me screamed to stop her,
but breaking cover meant exposure, and the Court
would know we were there.

Kael moved silent at my side, head tilted like
he was listening to the future.
Ciaran muttered under his breath, "This will end
badly for the witch. I can feel it."

"Shh," I hissed. "She'll hear."
The trees thinned.
We saw it,
the Gate.
We saw Ines shove Joanna through it.
And before I could think, before fear could win,
I leapt after her.

Ciaran

Of course, Zane jumped first.
He always had to play the hero,
that brooding, antlered idiot.
And me?
Of course I followed.
Not because I was brave.
Because I loved the witch.
And the idiot.
But even cowards follow the people they can't
lose.
So, I went too.

Joanna

Stone shattered around me.
My ribs screamed like splintered glass.

Pain ripped through my shoulder, white-hot and endless.
Grit filled my mouth.
Blood coated my tongue.
When I rolled onto my side, the air hit wrong, too thick, too wet, like breathing smoke.
The world pulsed gray.
And then—
her.
Morgan.

She was crumpled against the stone, folded in on herself.
Her skin the color of ash where blood hadn't reached.
Long gashes carved her face.
Her hair hung in ropes.
Purple bruises mottled her body.
Her ankle was mangled, bent at a grotesque angle.
A pool of crimson spread beneath her, slick and alive.
Beside her lay a nightmare beast,
lion's head, goat's body, serpent's tail,
its neck bent at an impossible angle.

A sharp rock lay in Morgan's blood-slick hand.

My heart split open.
Her lips were parted, dry and cracked.
She didn't move.
She didn't breathe.
Tears blurred my sight.
No.

I stumbled to her side, slipping in blood.
My hands slid through the warmth that was
leaving her.
I touched her hair, cold.

My fingers shook so violently I could barely
move it from her face.
Her chest was still.
"No. No. Gods, no, not you, Morgan. Please."
I pressed my palm to her sternum.
Nothing.

No heartbeat.

"Gods, please, Morgan, you can't be dead…"
A sob tore through me, raw and animal.
I folded over her, tears slicking her skin.
"You can't do this to me. Not like this. We didn't
even finish our story."

The words broke apart in my mouth. "No, no,
no…"
I pressed my forehead to hers, rocking her back
and forth,
blood soaking through my clothes,
grief cracking my ribs open.

"PLEASE, GODS, DON'T TAKE HER. TAKE ME
INSTEAD…"

I begged. I cursed. I wept.
The silence screamed back.
Then—
A flicker.
Her eyelids fluttered.
I froze.

A ragged breath scraped through her chest.
"…Morgan?"
My voice broke. "Morgan, gods—please."
She was *alive*.
Barely.
I gathered her up, blood hot on my arms.
Her head lolled heavy on my shoulder.
My knees threatened to give, but I kept moving.

A cave yawned nearby, black and wet. Shelter.

I stumbled inside and lowered her to the stone, my arms shaking.
I tore at my tunic, but the fabric wouldn't rip.
So I used my dagger.
The sound of tearing cloth was deafening.
I pressed the makeshift bandages down, blood slicking them before they even touched her wounds.
"Stay with me," I whispered, voice shredded.
"Please, Morgan. Stay."
Her chest rose shallow and slow, each breath weaker than the last.
Blood poured—hot, relentless—slipping through my fingers like water.
"Please, Morgan. Don't leave me like this."
My throat felt hollow.
The dagger clattered from my grip.
I bent over her instead, forehead to her clammy skin.
"Please, Morgan…"

Footsteps.
At the cave mouth.

My dagger snapped back into my hand,
Zane.
Relief hit like a wave.
"HELP ME!" I screamed. "PLEASE! I CAN'T
STOP THE BLEEDING—SHE'S DYING!"

Zane

I dropped to my knees beside them.
Joanna's face was streaked with tears, her hands
trembling, drenched in blood.
Morgan's body lay limp in her lap, pale and slick
with red.
For a moment, my stomach lurched.
I'd seen battlefields.
But not this.
"Move," I rasped. "I've got it."

I pressed my hands over hers, steady where
hers shook.
Tightened the knots I'd learned to make when
men bled out in my arms.
Morgan groaned once—a faint, broken sound—
and I clung to it like a prayer.
She was still here.
She had to be.

Joanna

It wasn't enough.

> Blood slicked my hands until it dripped from
> my wrists in thin red rivers.

> My tears mixed with it, streaking her skin with
> salt and sorrow.

Ciaran's voice cut sharp through the dark.

"You're wasting cloth."

I whipped around, chest heaving.

> He crouched near the shadows, pale and calm,
> a needle and thread glinting between his fingers
> like something obscene.

"If you can stitch clothes," he said evenly,
"you can stitch her."

My throat closed. "What?"

"Stitch her," he repeated. "You're the only one
who can."

For a second, I wanted to laugh,

because it sounded insane.

As if torn flesh were no different than mending
hems.

But Morgan's blood said otherwise.

It was everywhere.

It was slipping through my fingers faster than I could hold it back.

My stomach flipped.

My hands shook so badly I could barely hold the needle.

If I failed, she'd be gone by morning.

And it would be my fault.

I met Ciaran's eyes, and for once,

there was no humor in them at all.

"Do it," he said softly. "Or we lose her."

CHAPTER 29
Threads Unraveling
Kael

The cave was too loud in all the wrong ways.

Joanna's sobs tore through the stone,
cracked open and raw,
like the world had ended yesterday
and she was still kneeling in its ashes.

Zane's breathing followed, measured,
controlled,
the sound of a man built to carry too much
and finally wondering if this weight would break
him.

Ciaran's voice cut sharp,
little barbs flung in the air as if his words alone
could stitch faster than his hands.
And Morgan…
bleeding, shuddering,
tethered to a song only fools could mistake for
mercy.

I stayed silent.
My voice would only feed the chaos.

The threads spoke enough.

Threads never shut up.

They hum.
They pull.
They gnaw behind your teeth until you want to
bite through your own tongue
just to quiet them.
Joanna's thread was salt—
sharp and stinging,
like the mouthful of blood that comes after biting
down too hard.

Ashes and Steel

Morgan's was light—
blinding, brittle,
splintered glass that cut the hands holding it.

Together their tether should have made sense.
Two halves, one whole.
But it didn't.

It screamed.

Too bright.
Too taut.
Already unraveling.

I tilted my head, listening to the thrum.
They thought they were sewing flesh.

What they didn't realize was
they were forcing chaos into its seams,
patching at a prophecy—
and prophecies don't like to be patched.

The vision hit before I could brace for it—
cracked through me fast, jagged, unkind.

They always are.

• A Gate splitting wide, screaming with the sound
of stone breaking bone.
• Salt boiling the sea, skin blistering, lungs
flooding until bodies sank like anchors.
• Smoke twisting through ribs, snapping them like
twigs as it hollowed them out from the inside.
• Two crowns balanced on skulls half-buried in
the dirt,
    the grave beneath them still fresh

and still hungry.

Charming.

The witch and the fae.
Bound so tight they'd tear the world apart.

Not today.
Not tomorrow.
But soon.

I breathed in. Out.
The mask rasped it back—a cruel little echo.

Zane bent low, his hands steady as stone,
threading skin with the care of a soldier
who had stitched dying men a hundred times
and knew when it wouldn't matter.

Joanna rocked Morgan like she could shake breath
back into her lungs,
grief clawing at her voice until it turned almost
tender—
a lullaby sung through cracked ribs.

Ciaran smirked,
because smirking was safer than admitting
he cared enough to bleed for her.

And me?

I listened.

To the song no one else could hear.
To the threads unspooling like a noose in the
corners of the cave.

Time isn't straight.

It frays.
It folds.
It twists until it strangles itself.

Behind my eyes, visions looped like knots pulled
too tight—
each one sharper, each one crueler.

• A pyre, flames clawing up a woman's body
  while her scream turned hollow halfway
through.
• Clocks chiming in a place without walls,
  their faces split open, gears spilling like entrails.
• Hands reaching, veins bursting beneath the skin
  as they stretched too far—
  always too late,
  always *almost.*

Unraveling.

Ashes and Steel
Always unraveling.

I closed my eyes and let the echo settle.
The hum faded to a whisper—thin and knowing.

And like always…
I didn't tell them.

Why ruin the surprise?

CHAPTER 30
The Art of Finally
Joanna

The cave reeked of iron and wet stone.
My hands lunged for the thread.
They were slick with sweat, trembling so hard I
dropped the needle three times before I could
make it stay between my fingers.
Salt burned the corners of my mouth. My tears
wouldn't stop.

The flame beside us hissed each time a drop
fell.

I bent low until my forehead nearly brushed
Morgan's shoulder.
The smell of her blood was copper and smoke,
thick enough to taste.

"I... I can't—"

My voice broke like glass.
I shoved the needle at Zane.

He caught my hand mid-shake, steady and certain.
"I'll do it. It's okay."

The needle pierced flesh.
Morgan hissed through her teeth, a ragged
sound that split the quiet like lightning.
Her body jerked once, feathers twitching.
I almost tore Zane away, but the bleeding
slowed.

Each stitch was a tremor in the dark.
Skin tugged, stretched, then held.
Seam after seam, she held.

The stone floor stayed slick, blood seeping
between the cracks,

a warm stickiness crawling up my knees and
wrists.
My tunic clung to me, soaked through.
But at least the flow had slowed.

Minutes bled into hours.
The torch guttered low,
casting shadows that swayed like ghosts against
the walls.

My arms ached from holding her.
My eyes burned raw.
Her skin burned hotter, fever already creeping in.
I tore another strip from my tunic and soaked it in
the thin trickle of cave water that smelled of metal.
I pressed it to her brow, her neck, her chest.
Steam rose where it met her skin.

"Don't go," I whispered, voice cracking. "Please."

Her lashes trembled.
Her lips parted, chapped and bloody.

"Jo..." she rasped. "If I don't get to tell you... I love—"

Her words broke off.
Her head lolled.

"NO!" The sound clawed its way out of me.
I shook her, the motion splattering blood across my face.
"Morgan, no, you can't go! Not before I tell you..."

Ciaran grabbed my shoulders. His voice cut through like steel.
"She's not gone. She needs food. She's lost too much blood."

I tore through my pouch. My hands slipped, smashing the berries inside until the juice ran sticky between my fingers.
I pressed the pulp to her lips.
Purple smeared her mouth, running down her chin.

Nothing.
Just that awful stillness.

And then—
A cough.
Small. Wet. Living.

Her body jerked, and air ripped back into her
lungs.
"Gods, Jo…" she croaked, eyes fluttering open.
"That tastes disgusting."

The sound of her voice shattered me.
A sob-laugh burst out, ugly and beautiful all at
once.
Tears streamed freely now, streaking down onto
her skin.

"I love you."
It fell out before I could catch it,
like it had been waiting under my tongue this
whole time.

Her expression froze; shock, disbelief, something
dangerously soft.

"I mean it," I said again, louder. "You were

delirious. You were going to say it anyway. But I love you. I LOVE YOU."

Her lips parted.
And she whispered back.

"I love you too, Jo."

For half a heartbeat, I didn't believe her.

Morgan

The words slipped free before I could stop them.
They hung in the air, shimmering like heat off stone.

Her head turned toward me,
eyes wide, mouth open, shaking.
She looked like she was watching a star crash to earth.

"Say that again," she whispered.

"Joanna?"

"No." Her hand trembled as it hovered near my arm. "Please. I need you to say it again."

My chest hurt, my throat raw, but the truth clawed its way out.
"I love you, Joanna."

Her breath hitched.
She leaned her forehead against mine, grounding us both.
Her fingers slid to my wrists—
not to restrain, but to keep me here.

"One more time," she whispered, her voice breaking. "I need to feel you mean it."

The words ripped out, feral and cracked.

"I LOVE YOU, JOANNA!
Do I need to scream it from the rooftops?
I loved you from the moment I saw you in my dreams.
I loved you when you caught me talking to that damned rug.
I loved you when you dragged me out of the Court

like some witchy knight in shining armor.

And I'll love you forever—until my last breath
burns out."

She laughed, shaking.
"You almost died, you idiot. But I love you even
more for it."

Joanna

Her tunic was ruined, soaked through with blood.
When I peeled it back to clean her, my fingers
brushed her back—
and froze.

The skin there was uneven.
Raised. Hard.

Scars.

I traced the lines with shaking fingers.
Rough ridges, twin tracks carved where wings
once lived.

Torn out, healed over wrong.
I felt every inch of it like a confession.

Tears blurred my sight. They spilled onto her
shoulders, darkening the fabric.
"Gods, Morgan… you shouldn't have had to
survive this. What did they do to you?"

She turned her face away, eyes closed tight.
A single tear slid from the corner.

Then I saw it,
a brand burned deep between her shoulder blades,
a sigil twisted into her flesh.
It shimmered faintly in the firelight.

My stomach flipped.
I pressed my palm over it as if pressure could
erase it.

"No. No, no, no. What is this? Why would
anyone—"

She didn't answer.
She just trembled.

I kissed her temple, whispering,
"I've got you. You're safe now. I love you even
with these."

Morgan

That anyone could love me, *me*, branded, broken,
and bleeding
felt impossible.

I wanted to vanish into the stone.
But Joanna held me tighter, her heartbeat
hammering against mine.
Like she was daring the gods to take me again.

The weight of it cracked me open.
Tears slid silent down my cheeks.
For the first time in years, they didn't burn.

And then—

Clap.
Sharp.
Too sharp.

Clap.
Slower.
Mocking.

Clap.
The last one echoed,
each beat vibrating through the stone walls.

From the Shadows, Ines.

Her smile was wrong.
Too perfect.
Too still.

She dragged her nails down the wall as she stepped forward,
each scrape slicing through the quiet like a blade.
Every tap of her heel followed in rhythm.

"Bravo," she purred.
"Truly beautiful. Thank you for keeping my little pet warm for me."

The word *pet* detonated in my skull.
The air vanished from my lungs.
My stomach twisted.

Before I could think, I was crawling backward—
palms slipping in blood,
heels skidding against stone.
Retreat. Recoil. Hide.

The scent of her perfume—jasmine and iron—
filled the cave.
It choked me.

Joanna

For a heartbeat, I couldn't move.
Ines's voice slithered through the air like smoke
through a wound.

When I turned, her eyes were on Morgan.
Her grin glimmered, predatory.
The cave light made her skin look unreal, silvered
like bone.

I looked back at Morgan.

She was shaking, wings folded tight, arms
around her chest.
Her face was all shame and silence.

323

Something inside me broke in two.

My jaw locked.
My grief hardened into something else—
something sharp and blinding.

"YOU."
The word shot out like a spark.
"You think you can walk in here and act like
you didn't take what wasn't yours?"

Ines tilted her head, the gesture snake-smooth.
"Oh, but I had permission," she said, eyes glinting.
Her smile grew, delicate and cruel.
"Isn't that right, little pet?"

Morgan's head dipped lower.
Her silence was answer enough.

Rage bloomed hot under my skin.
"She's not your pet."

Ines laughed—a low, dragging sound like silk
tearing over stone.
"Not mine?" she echoed, voice sweet as poison.

"Sweet witch, she wears my marks. She's bound to me, whether she claws at the binding or not."

She tilted her head again, eyes half-lidded. "Don't worry, little witch. The Court is already on its way.
You and your fae will be together soon enough..."

She stepped closer, boots whispering through the blood.

"...already caged."

And I knew,
we were trapped.

CHAPTER 31
The Silence Between
Joanna

The silence stretched long,
too long.

Not the kind that waits.
The kind that *listens back.*

It pressed down on us, heavy and absolute, until
even the sound of my own breath scraped against
it.
Each inhale felt like betrayal. Each exhale, a
warning.

Something was wrong.
The kind of wrong that doesn't arrive, it's already here.

I wanted to run.
Gods, I wanted to move, to grab Morgan by the wrist and drag her toward the cave mouth—
but the air was already thick with the scent of endings.

Then it hit.
Taste first—metallic, bitter.
Iron coated my tongue like I'd bitten through my own mouth.

Magic.
Old. Rotten.
Not the kind that hummed or breathed, but the kind that *remembered* how to chain things.

"MORGAN!"

My voice cracked through the stillness.
The echo hit the walls, then died—like even sound was afraid to linger.

Morgan braced on her hands, trembling.
She tried to stand. Her knees buckled.

The bandages around her stomach darkened red, leaking through the fabric.
She fell again, breath hitching sharp.

Zane moved before I did.
He was all motion and muscle, no hesitation, no sound, just pure instinct.

He caught her mid-fall, hauling her against his chest as if she weighed nothing.
The veins in his neck stood out. His jaw locked so tight it looked carved from stone.
His eyes, gods, those eyes were pure fire, fixed on the dark ahead, on what was coming.
He knew.

Ciaran cursed under his breath, low and vicious.
The sound of it cut through the quiet like a blade drawn slow.
He spun, his hand twitching for a weapon he knew wouldn't be enough.
"Run," he snarled, but even he heard how hollow it sounded.

Kael didn't move.
He lingered near the cave mouth, mask tilted, head cocked as though listening for a pulse buried in the dark.
The shadows at his boots writhed like restless serpents, curling in anticipation.

And Ines,
Ines only smiled.

Her nails dragged down the wall, the sound high and deliberate, each scrape tracing my spine like cold fingers.
When she spoke, her voice purred low and satisfied.
"They're here."

Then the world broke open.

Stone *screamed*.
The sound was ribs cracking, the cave itself splitting wide.
Light detonated through the tunnel, a violent bloom of white so sharp it carved pain behind my eyes.

Dust hit like a wave.
It filled my mouth, my lungs.
I coughed, but the air was grit and metal.
My tongue tasted like blood.

And beneath it, footsteps.

Dozens.
Hundreds.
Boots striking stone in perfect rhythm.

The kind of rhythm that belonged to trained killers.

The sound ricocheted through the cave, echo to echo, until it was impossible to count them.
It filled the space between heartbeats.

The light shifted.
Shapes moved inside the haze.
And then they stepped through.

Enforcers.

Their robes slashed in crimson, their shoulders armored in blackened iron, faces half-hidden in shadow.
Sigils glowed faintly across their chests—blue and

sharp, pulsing like veins under skin.
The air around them bent, warped, reeking of
scorched salt and iron.

The ground itself shuddered as one slammed
his staff down.
Cracks split the floor, spiderwebbing outward,
humming with runes that crawled toward our
boots.
My skin prickled.
The air burned cold.
Every nerve lit up like fire trying to be ice.

Zane adjusted Morgan higher against him,
shielding her with his body.
Blood streaked down his arms. His breath came
rough, but his stance was unbreakable.

Ciaran stood a few feet to the side, grin too
sharp, too bright, his armor against fear.
He flipped his blade in one hand, a reckless light
dancing behind his eyes.
"Gods," he muttered, "I hate it when I'm right."

Kael's whisper barely touched the air.
A single word.

The shadows near him deepened, twitching, reaching.

And me,
I could feel the fire rising inside my bones.

It started at the base of my spine, heat curling upward, crackling through my ribs like something alive.
My heartbeat thudded heavy against it,
fire against panic.

Magic built in my throat.
It wanted out.
It *begged* to burn.

Then came another sound,
faint at first.
Behind us.

More boots.
Closer.
Dozens. Maybe more.

The cave threw their echoes back at us in cruel repetition until I couldn't tell which way was forward anymore.

The air turned claustrophobic, buzzing.
My pulse matched their steps.

We were surrounded.
Trapped between two jaws closing.

Zane's knuckles went white around his sword.
Ciaran exhaled through a shaky laugh.
Kael's mask tilted, the runes on it flaring once—
as if even he knew the pattern of our deaths had
already been written.

And Ines,
Ines simply stepped aside.
Her smile was all invitation.

The light flashed again, brighter this time.
A sound like thunder—like the sky splitting in
two.
And then the first Enforcer lunged through the
haze.

There was no escape.
No running.
No fighting.

Only *falling*.

CHAPTER 32
The Chains of the broken
Morgan

Zane's arms locked around me, steady as iron—
his heartbeat thudding against my cheek, a drum I could almost keep time with.
For a single heartbeat, I almost believed I was safe.
Anchored.
Held.

But each step he took ripped fire through my stitches.
Every jolt sawed a blade through my stomach, tearing me open from the inside.
My body was failing; I could feel the seams giving way.

Still he held me tighter, as if the rhythm of his chest could breathe back into mine.

Then the Councilors stepped out of the dark.

Red robes dusted with ash.
Iron masks dull and pitiless.
Their presence alone warped the air—pressure thickening until the cavern itself felt alive and cruel.
Magic pressed down like the hand of a god.
The air vibrated, low and electric. Even the stone shuddered under its weight.

"Hand her over," Veridias barked, voice cracking through the dark like struck metal.

Zane's jaw clenched; cords stood sharp in his neck. He didn't loosen his hold. Didn't blink. "She won't last if you…"

They didn't let him finish.

Two magisters lunged.
Hands of bone and steel ripped me from his arms.
Their grip was merciless, tearing me free so violently the world flashed white.
Pain exploded through every nerve—pure,

blinding, total.

The scream caught in my throat, crushed half-silent beneath the iron collar, but it burned its way out anyway, a strangled sob that wasn't quite human.

"NO!"

Joanna's cry split the cavern open.
Raw. Animal.
She was feral—collared, shackled, but still *fighting*.
She clawed one magister's mask, raking crimson across the steel.
Another grabbed her shoulders—she sank her teeth into his wrist until blood slicked the floor.
They slammed her down, chains biting, but she kept thrashing, and kept screaming my name like sound itself could pull me back to her.

Zane charged again, rage distilled into motion.
His fist cracked across a jaw, bone snapped, teeth skittered across the floor.
For a breath, just one heartbeat, his arms were around me again.
Fierce. Desperate. Unyielding.

Then a chain snapped through the air.
The sound was thunder.

It coiled around his chest, glowing white with
spell-fire, and yanked him backward.
The impact rattled the cavern; his back hit stone
hard enough to crack it.
The sound, *that* sound, stayed in me.
He slumped, breath gone, but his arm still reached
toward me. Always reaching.

I was slammed onto the floor.
Stone met bone, and something in me tore.
The wound split wide, blood spilling hot and slick
beneath me.
Hands forced my arms out, and the black steel
cuffs clamped down—
cold like nothing living, hollow like it drank the air
itself.

The metal bit through skin, down to bone,
and then it *fed*.

The chill crept inward, through my veins, into
my lungs, crawling up my spine.
It gnawed. It *hungered*.

My magic stuttered, then died, strangled at its source.

Joanna's voice still cut through.
"DON'T TOUCH HER! Don't you *dare!*"

Her throat shredded the words raw. Blood
flecked her lips.
Three enforcers pinned her down, knees grinding
into her spine.
She fought anyway, eyes locked on mine, blazing
and breaking all at once.

Ciaran spat curses that sparked like flint.
A boot to his ribs silenced him with a dull crack.
Kael's head tilted; his masked voice was calm as
winter.
"Threads tangle. Threads break."

The cuffs sealed with a hiss.
Cold swallowed me whole.

The last thing I saw before the dark folded over us
was Joanna's face,
bloodied, feral, shining with tears,
as they dragged us apart.

Later,

The world jolted back as the wagon lurched forward.
Wood groaned. Iron screamed.
Wheels scraped stone with the sound of bone grinding against bone.

> The air was thick,
> iron, blood, and damp rot.
> Suppression wards pulsed through the space like a heartbeat, slow and cruel, squeezing the breath out of us.

They threw Joanna in first.
Her body hit the floor with a sick thud.
That sound tore through me worse than the chains.

> Then they threw me.
I landed against her before I could stop myself.
Even bound, I turned until my forehead found hers.
Her skin was clammy, her lips pale—but warm enough that I knew she was still breathing.
Just breathing.

I clung to that.
It was the only thing left to hold.

Her lashes trembled, a half-dream flicker.
She didn't speak. Just the rasp of breath in the
dark.

Zane came next, hurled in like a sack of stone.
Blood ran from his temple, a crimson trail down
his cheek.
He dragged himself to the wall, chains scraping,
settling between us like a guard dog still ready to
bite.
His hand hovered close to Joanna, protective even
in ruin.

Ciaran followed, laughing through blood, the
sound cracked and brittle.
"Chains and collars," he rasped. "How original."
A staff slammed into his jaw. The laughter cut
short.

Kael entered last—
unforced.
The guards didn't dare touch him.
He stepped inside like he belonged there, mask

catching the thin slit of light between the boards.

"The tether strains," he whispered. "Soon it will snap."

The wagon rattled on.
Hours. Maybe days.
No sun. No sky.
Only the churn of wheels and the quiet sounds of people trying not to die.

Joanna's breathing hitched every few minutes. Zane muttered curses under his breath, the sound of a man bargaining with gods who weren't listening.
Ciaran groaned and laughed in the same breath.
Kael hummed something that didn't sound like a song.

I didn't sleep.
Couldn't.

The black steel gnawed slow, chewing through me, hollowing me out bite by bite.
It fed. I weakened.
Every second, it took more, magic, warmth,

341

thought.
Even my heartbeat slowed, quieter, until I could
barely hear it.

When the wheels stopped, the silence was
almost tender.
Almost.

Then the light slashed in.
Blinding.

Hands grabbed us, rough and efficient.
They dragged Joanna first; she cried out, hoarse
and raw, her collar chain pulling tight.
Zane thrashed next, wild and silent, until three
men bore him down.
Ciaran spat blood in a magister's face and earned a
boot to the ribs for it.

They saved me for last.

Two magisters hauled me by the arms,
I was too weak to fight, barely breathing.
My knees scraped stone, skin splitting open again.
When they threw me down, the cuffs burned
hotter, devouring what little was left of me.

Then the walls moved in.

One cell.

They shoved Joanna through first.
She stumbled, caught herself on the wall.
Then me.
My knees hit the ground, and I collapsed against
her, forehead brushing her shoulder.
The chains clinked between us, cold and intimate.

Zane and Ciaran were dragged in after.
Kael followed without a hand laid on him.

The door slammed.
Iron screamed against iron.

Darkness swallowed us whole.

And beneath it all,
I felt the chains hum,
a slow, steady pulse, feeding, breathing, *waiting.*

That was when I understood.
The hunger of chains wasn't just the metal.
It was alive.

And it was starving.

CHAPTER 33

The corridor wept in rhythm.
Each drop of water fell from the ceiling and struck stone like a heartbeat counting down.
Drip.
Drip.
Drip.
Every sound echoed through the spine of the keep, down to where they kept her—my ruin, my creation.

The air stank of damp iron and old blood, heavy enough to breathe in. Every inhale tasted like rust. Every exhale curled smoke-thick against the torchlight.

> My boots struck the floor with precision:
> *Click.*
> *Click.*
> *Click.*
> A procession of control. Regal. Slow. The sound of someone who never hurries because she always arrives.

The guards didn't meet my eyes. They stood back, bodies stiff with the kind of fear that hums through the bones. They wouldn't enter. They knew better.

> The cell hummed before I even touched it. Suppression wards thrummed under the skin of the stone, seeping into marrow. The air itself felt drugged. Dead.

I dragged my fingers across the bars—cold enough to sting. Sparks flared faint and blue where my nails scraped the sigils.

When I pushed, the iron screamed.
And I stepped inside.

Morgan

The chains sang every time I breathed.
Metal grinding against metal.
Too loud. Too sharp.

My wrists were fire. The cuffs had rubbed the
skin raw until I could feel bone under the
slickness. My ankles throbbed, carved deep with
bruises where the shackles bit. My throat burned
with copper from screaming earlier, my voice long
gone, swallowed by stone.

Then I heard it.
Click.
Click.
Click.
That rhythm that haunted dreams.

The smell hit next, spice, smoke, a sweetness that
soured the air.
Familiar. Poisonous.
It slithered through the cell like perfume spilled
over rot.

My body went rigid.
Every muscle locked. Every breath hitched.
Oh gods. It's her.

Her shadow came before her. Long. Twisted.
Crawling across the floor until it touched me, cold
as a grave.

> The torchlight bent around her when she
> entered, gilding her edges in gold that wasn't
> light but mockery.
> I wanted to vanish. To dissolve. To become
> dust.

"Morgan."

> She said my name like she owned it.
> The sound slid through the cell, syrup-slow,
> cutting deep before I could flinch.

My back hit stone, hard enough to knock the air
out of me. The wall was slick with condensation. It
soaked into my tunic. I could feel every heartbeat
against it, my own pulse ricocheting through the
cold.

> She crouched. Close enough that her breath
> brushed my cheek.
> It smelled like honey gone bad.

Her gloved finger tilted my chin up. The leather was soft, but the pressure wasn't. It was control dressed as care.

"Don't be so sad, little puppet," she cooed. Her smile didn't reach her eyes. "It's all right. We can show them what we do in private."

Her words tasted like smoke in my mouth.

I shook my head once. Twice. The chains bit deep, clinking against the floor, the sound too intimate. My throat closed.

She leaned closer. "Come now, little pet. Show them. Show *her*. Now."

Her voice slid inside me like silk soaked in venom.
The magic beneath it twisted the air.
My breath broke.
My body betrayed me again.
My lips parted, unwilling.

And I tilted my chin upward.

Joanna

Oh gods.

She kissed her.

Morgan kissed *her*.

The sound of it was soft, flesh against flesh, a wet whisper that sliced through the stillness.
And it burned.
It burned so badly it hollowed me out from the inside.

The world went quiet in that terrible, ringing way that happens right before screaming.

The air turned metallic.
The smell of blood and fear mixed into something bitter on my tongue.

Her lips moved against Ines's like prayer and surrender and madness all at once. Her lashes fluttered. The noise she made, a strangled half-sob, half-moan,
it didn't sound like pain.

My stomach twisted into knots.
The tether inside me coiled, convulsed, and split.

One tear slid down my cheek. It felt *hot*. Too hot. It burned the way betrayal always does.

Zane roared first.
"GET OFF HER!"
The chains rattled like thunder as he yanked against them. Blood ran bright down his forearms.

Ciaran spat, sparks jumping and dying at his feet. "Monster," he hissed.

But I couldn't speak. Couldn't move.
I just stood there. Watching. Breaking.

The kiss shattered something sacred.

And when Ines finally pulled away, Morgan's breath stuttered, slow, trembling, like she'd forgotten how to breathe without her.

That was the moment I stopped believing in anything good.

The word *convenient* rang again in my head, cruel as laughter.
And I believed it.

Because she chose Ines.
Because she didn't stop her.

The tether writhed in my chest.
I tasted iron, real blood from biting down too hard.

I wanted to scream. I wanted to claw the air apart.
But my knees gave out instead.
The weight of it, love, rage, grief, collapsed me.

Nothing had ever hurt this much.

Ines

I pulled back slowly, savoring the aftermath.
The taste of fear. The tremor under her skin. The silence that followed.

Her pupils were wide, her lips still parted, her breath catching like she'd run a mile.

I smiled.

Leaning close, my lips brushed her ear.
My voice came out soft, almost kind.
"You're still mine."

She flinched.

Then, louder, so the witch would hear, so they *all* would:

"See, witch? She'll *always* be mine."

I smiled wider. "And you can't stop it."

CHAPTER 34
The Body Remembers
Joanna

The door slammed shut with a crack that rattled the stone.
The echo lingered too long.

Ines's laughter curled through the air—smoke-thin and sweet as decay. It wrapped around my throat like a noose that didn't tighten but waited.

The silence that followed wasn't peace.
It was the silence that hums right before a scream.

My stomach churned.
That kiss replayed, over and over—wet, wrong,
real. I could still hear it, still *taste* it in the air, sharp
and salt-sweet.
My body wouldn't let it go.

I turned on her.

Morgan lay curled on the floor, wrists bound,
shoulders trembling. Blood seeped through the
seams of her tunic, black in the dim light. Her face
was turned away, pressed against the stone like
she wanted it to swallow her.

She smelled of sweat, blood, and that
godsforsaken spice that clung to her skin, Ines's
scent. It made me sick.

"Gods damn you."

The words came out cracked and feral.

Zane flinched, raising his hands. "Jo, don't.
You don't know what she's capable of…"

"Don't you dare tell me what I know."
My voice hit like flint against steel.

I stepped closer. The air between us burned.

"I saw you," I hissed. "Not Ines. YOU."

Her eyes lifted, wet, glassy, pleading.

It should have softened me. It didn't.

"You think I've forgotten?"
My voice rose, trembling with fury and
heartbreak all tangled into one.
"How you left me tied to that chair like I was
nothing? What if I hadn't gotten out? What if I
had burned alive?"

Her lips parted, the faintest whisper of my name.

I cut it down.

"You stole my mother's memory like it was
yours to keep. You mocked me. You made me feel
small. And then, then, you called me a
convenience."

The words were ash in my mouth, bitter and final.

Her mouth trembled. "Jo…"

"DON'T."

It tore out like lightning, loud enough to make
Ciaran flinch.

"You said it yourself," I spat. "I was just a warm body. A convenience."

The silence that followed didn't feel like silence. It felt like suffocating.

The cell reeked of blood and rot and despair. The iron chains hummed faintly under the torchlight, warm where the heat met cold. Sweat slicked my palms. My breath came ragged.

And she,
she folded in on herself, trembling.
Her hair clung to her face, damp with sweat and tears.

I could still smell Ines on her.
Sweet. Spiced. Poison.

Zane turned away, jaw tight.
Ciaran muttered a prayer through his teeth that sounded more like a curse.

Morgan whispered something I didn't hear.
Maybe my name. Maybe sorry.
I didn't care.

She looked so small, curled up in the dark.
And that—more than the kiss, more than the
words—made me hate her most.

Because the body remembers.

And mine remembered betrayal.

CHAPTER 35
What was Taken
Morgan

I…"

The word snagged in my throat like glass. My mouth filled with the taste of copper before I even realized I was bleeding it. "Jo, I can explain."

Her head snapped toward me, eyes rimmed in red, lashes wet and trembling. Her voice came sharp enough to cut.

"Don't give me excuses."

Her shoulders shook. "Not after what I just saw."

The air between us burned. My chest collapsed under it. Still, the words clawed their way out— ragged, uneven, desperate.

"It's not what you think. It's not wanted. It's not love. Gods, Jo, please, just listen."

She didn't move. Didn't blink. The silence between us stretched taut as a garrote.

So, I kept talking. Because if I stopped, I'd shatter.

"I… gods, Jo…" My voice shook like a snapped bowstring. "I tied you down like you were nothing. I walked away. I left you. I stole things that weren't mine—pieces of you I had no right to touch. Your toy… your mother's memory…" My throat caught; the next breath scraped raw. "I should've known what it meant. I didn't. I mocked you when I should've protected you. I pushed you away when you were the only one who stayed. I told you that you were a convenience, a warm body because

I thought if I made you hate me enough, you'd leave. You'd be safe."

My breath broke. "But all I did was destroy you."

The chains bit into my wrists as I shifted. Blood slicked the metal, the smell sharp in the stale air. "Jo, I'm sorry. For every wound I left in you. For every word that cut when it shouldn't have. For every time you thought you were nothing to me. You weren't."

My voice splintered into something small and wrecked.
"You never were."

Joanna

Her apology hit like a wave I didn't want to drown in.
I stood there, heartbeat stuttering against my ribs, and waited for something, anything to sound like the truth.

But one thing stayed burning, unanswered.

"I appreciate your apology," I whispered, the words tasting like iron. "But it doesn't explain one thing."

My voice hardened.
"Why did you kiss her? Why did you let her touch you—after everything—and right in front of me?"

Morgan

My body jolted. The question hit harder than any whip.

"I..." My voice cracked on the first syllable. "I didn't..." The next breath came out broken, like I'd swallowed smoke. "I didn't want to, Jo. I swear it. I didn't want it."

My chest locked up. The words scraped raw as they clawed their way out.

"She took my wings."
The memory ripped through me before I could stop it.
"She cut them off me like they were nothing.

She branded me where they'd been. She said I was hers, and gods, she made it true."

My knees buckled; the chains caught me mid-collapse. I pressed my forehead to the floor, cold stone biting against my skin.

"She rewired me, Jo." The confession bled out, shaking. "Every strike, every, every touch, she twisted it. Until I didn't know the difference between pain and obedience. Until my body didn't belong to me anymore."

The words came faster now, unraveling. "So, when she touched me—when she kissed me—my body remembered. It *obeyed.* It betrayed me. It betrayed *you.*"

I choked on a sob. "She left something in me, Jo. Something I can't scrape out. When she took my wings, she carved a mark into me, a bond." I lifted my head, meeting her eyes through the blur of tears. "It ties me to her. If I fight it, it crushes me from the inside. My ribs, my lungs, my heart, everything. It feels like drowning in my own bones."

I tried to breathe, but my lungs rasped shallow, desperate. "So, when she said, 'show them,' I couldn't stop it. My body moved before my mind. It wasn't me."

My voice dissolved into a whisper. "She stole my will, Jo. That's what you saw. Not love. No choice. What was taken."

Joanna

I stared at her, at the tears streaking her cheeks, the tremor in her hands.
Part of me wanted to believe her.
But the ache in my chest burned hotter than pity.

"No."
The word cracked sharp, echoing against the stone.

"There's no such magic," I said, my voice shaking but loud. "Not one that makes you kiss her. Not one that makes you look at her like that."

My throat burned with the taste of old salt.
"You want me to believe a spell can crawl

inside your body and make you betray me?" I spat. "That's not magic, Morgan. That's *you*."

Her face broke open, eyes wide, wet, pleading.

Zane's voice cut through, low and steady. "She's telling the truth, Jo. I've seen it. The bond, it breaks her apart when she fights it."

Ciaran's voice rasped from the shadows. "Old magic," he said, like a curse. "Chains in the marrow. No one fights it and lives."

But their words only twisted the knife.

I crossed my arms tight, forcing the tears back. "You think I'm a fool?" My voice trembled, but I didn't stop. "That I'll swallow whatever you say because it's tragic enough to sound true? Because your friends stand beside you?"

Morgan's lips parted, trembling around words that couldn't find air.

I shook my head, tears stinging hot. "No," I whispered. "I saw you. I *heard* you."

I stepped back, choking on the taste of rust and grief. "That's not a bond. That's betrayal."

Morgan

The word *betrayal* shattered against me like glass.

I sagged where I knelt, chains groaning. The stone beneath me felt alive, throbbing with the echo of her voice, her fury, her heartbreak.

Jo turned away. Arms crossed, her face half-shadow, jaw set tight. Her magic flickered faint and cold across her skin—like a storm held at bay by sheer will.

She wouldn't look at me.

And I—
I couldn't stop looking at her.

Her hair stuck to her neck in the humidity, her shoulders shaking, her breath uneven. I wanted to tell her she was right to hate me. That I'd rather her fury than her pity. But no words came.

Only the soft rattle of chains.

Only the scent of blood, sweat, and smoke clinging to both of us.

And the silence.
That heavy, endless silence that made every
heartbeat sound like a scream.

Joanna

I stared into the dark until my vision blurred.
If I looked at her again, I'd break.
And gods help me—I didn't know whether I'd run
to her or kill her.

Behind me, she shook—quiet, contained, wrecked.

Her apology still lingered in the air between us.
But so did the sound of that kiss.
And nothing she said could make one erase the
other.

Morgan

I stayed there, hunched in the corner, the chains
biting deeper, the truth still bleeding out of me.

And none of it was enough.

Chapter 36

The things I saw

Joanna

She really kissed Ines.
She *really* kissed her in front of me.

And then she had the audacity to apologize,
like "sorry" could scrape the image from my head,
could bleach the memory of her lips pressed
against that monster. Like repentance was a
solvent strong enough to dissolve betrayal.

Then the explanation came.
No, not an explanation. A story. A myth. Another
Morgan-tragedy. A curse. A "bond." A new reason
to turn her into the victim again.

Always Morgan.

Always broken.

Always clawing sympathy out of the wreckage she caused.

She could've just *owned it*. Could've said, *yes, I kissed her,* could've looked me in the eye and admitted that some piece of her still belonged to Ines.

But no. She shoved it onto magic. Onto fate. Onto anything but herself.

And I'm supposed to sit here and believe it.

The taste of bile crawled up the back of my throat. My hands shook against my knees. The cell reeked of damp stone, blood, and burned metal. Her scent—salt, smoke, and something sweet that used to mean safety, made me nauseous.

"You wouldn't want me to be another warm body, would you?" My voice came out venom-slick, trembling but sharp. "Another *convenience*?"

Morgan

Gods—no.
Not that.

The word hit like a blade under the ribs.
I'd already apologized. I'd bled for it. Why
couldn't she *hear* me? Why couldn't she believe
me?

I love her. I would *never*—

But she doesn't see me.
She only sees betrayal.

Something cracked inside my chest. The ache
curdled into rage, into shame, into something too
sharp to swallow.

"Better a convenience than you," I spat. The
chains rattled as I surged forward, metal biting
into raw wrists. "Clinging to your mother's corpse
because it's the only love you'll ever know."

Joanna

My breath stopped.
The air froze in my throat, heavy as ash.

She said it. She went *there.*

Fine.
If she wanted blood, she'd get it.

"At least I can *love!*" I screamed, my voice
shredding as it ricocheted through the stone.
"YOU? You kiss anyone who fucking breathes.
LENA. INES. Who's next, CIARAN? Whore suits
you better than martyr!"

The air quivered.
Zane's voice cracked through it like a whip.

"Exactly!" he barked. "You parade around like
some tragic hero, but you're nothing but a Fae
whore, kissing anyone, including me, just for
attention! You kissed me, Morgan. Like none of it
mattered."

Morgan

My head snapped toward him. Fury flared white-hot.

"Yeah?" My voice dropped to a snarl. "And it was the kiss of a *wet dog*. You knew I wasn't straight, and you *still* kissed me. You're worse than Ines."

Joanna

That name, *her* name, coming from Morgan's lips again snapped something loose in me.

"YOU DISGUST ME!" I screamed, voice cracking but unstoppable. "You beg me to believe you, but all you ever give me are lies. Bonds, brands, old magic, anything but the truth! You kissed her because you *wanted* to. Just like you kissed him. Just like you'll kiss the next one who offers."

Zane growled, deep and guttural. "You don't know what Ines can do, Jo. I've seen the bond. I've seen it *rip her apart.*"

I laughed, short, sharp, cruel. "Of course you'd defend her. You had her lips on you too. Guess she gets around."

Zane's face darkened, eyes flashing murder.

Morgan

The rage ripped through me. My chest burned like wildfire under my ribs. The chains groaned with every heave of breath.

"Gods, Jo, you really aren't any better than Ines," I spat. "You talk about love like it's holy, but you weaponize it the same way she does. You think you're better than me? You *watched.* You sat there while they tied me up, while they dragged me away—and you did *nothing.*"

My gaze swung to the others, voice a snarl. "And you, both of you." The words trembled like thunder barely caged. "You bowed. You dropped

372

your heads to the dirt while they whipped me, carved me, and threw me into the Gate. Don't you dare talk to me about cowardice when you folded like reeds."

Zane's glare cut back at me. "You see what the Court can do, and you *still* don't believe Ines could have forced you?"

"Shut up, Zane!" I roared. "You don't get to come to my defense now. You, *both of you*, knew what she was doing. You knew she was breaking me, and you *let* her."

Ciaran

My voice sliced through their shouting like a knife. "You don't get to hurl your pain like stones and expect us to stand at your altar." I pointed at Zane, voice sharp as glass. "And you—you've got the emotional range of a toad."

Zane

"At least I don't laugh at other people's pain!" I snapped back. "You lost your wife and turned grief into a fucking punchline!"

Ciaran

The humor bled out of me fast. "Take that back," I hissed, voice shaking. "At least I don't walk around pretending to be a hero while rotting inside because my brothers never loved me."

Morgan

"ALL OF YOU, SHUT UP!"
The scream tore through my chest so hard the sound cracked the air itself. The cave trembled, dust raining from the ceiling. The chains rattled like thunder.

"You don't get to be this callous about pain," I shouted, voice raw, shaking. "Not after everything. You know what's been done to us. To *me.* And you still stand there cutting each other open."

Joanna

"That's rich," I hissed. "Coming from the one who weaponized my grief, who tied me up and called me convenient."

And that was it.
All of us screaming. All of us breaking.
The cell became a battlefield made of sound—
every word a wound, every breath a confession we'd regret.

Chains clanged. Dust fell. The air smelled of iron, salt, and rot.
Our voices bounced off the walls until it felt like the room itself was screaming back.

And then—

The door groaned.
The noise stopped cold.

"…What the fuck is going on?"

Lena

She stood in the doorway, boots slick with rain, hair matted, eyes wide. A torch burned behind her, throwing a warped halo of light into the chaos. She blinked at us, the wreckage, the blood, the tears, and tilted her head.

"Well," she said finally. "Guess I picked the wrong time to visit."

Joanna

I spun toward her, breath still shaking. "Perfect," I snapped. "Someone else for Morgan to kiss."

Lena blinked once, then that familiar half-smirk tugged at her mouth.
"Well. At least I'm cute."

For a beat, no one breathed.

Then, Ciaran snorted.

Zane swore under his breath.

Morgan let out a choked, broken laugh that turned halfway into a sob.

I wiped my face with the back of my hand, voice hollow but sharp.

"Well… if we're handing out partners, I call dibs on whoever brings snacks."

The cave fell into bitter, fractured laughter, cracked and hollow, like something dying trying to pretend it was still alive.

The echo lingered long after the sound was gone.

CHAPTER 37

The portal shimmered like a wound.
A dark mirror suspended in air, its surface
rippling with the hiss of wards, whispering secrets
in a tongue only I remembered. Every breath that
brushed its glass stank of ozone and blood magic,
the scent of things that had been bled into
obedience.

And within it, my masterpiece.

Morgan.

Through her reflection I saw it all: the cell, the
witch, the fae, the filth that called themselves her
friends. Every flicker of torchlight, every quiver of

378

their trembling mouths, every echo off the slick stone walls. The sound muffled, warped through the glass, first a murmur, then a chorus of rising shouts. Accusations. Cries. A symphony of chaos.

I drank it in.

Their rage was wine.
Their pain, music.
And Morgan... my perfect little ruin, caught in the middle, shaking like a candle drowning in its own wax.

The witch finally saw her for what she was. Feral. Not some tragic heroine, but a trembling, desperate little storm pretending to be human.

Morgan was never more than what I made her.
Scrap and bone and obedience.
A weapon wearing skin.
A slut carved from devotion.

I smiled. Gods, what beautiful noise they made. All of them ruthless. All of them animal.

And me?
I waited.

Still as stone. Patient as rot. Let them scream. Let them tear each other apart. Sooner or later, one of them would falter, and she would come crawling back.

Because Morgan never belonged to the witch.
She never belonged to *them*.
She belongs to *me*.

> To the Court.
> To the leash beneath her skin.
> To the sound of my voice when I whisper her name.

The mirror pulsed once, alive under my palm.

Their shouting cracked into silence for the span of a heartbeat. Then — that girl.

Lena.

Of course. The useless one. The healer who failed to heal, the friend who mistook pity for courage. Always stumbling into what was not hers.

She entered with a smirk, with that pathetic joke of hers, and they laughed.

Laughter.

> The sound rattled the glass. It echoed wrong. It was *mine*.

And then Morgan flinched.

> When I appeared, she flinched.

At me.

At *me*.

A low hum rose in my throat. The wards flickered blue. The mirror hissed under my hand.

Oh, I will make her pay for that.

> Every gasp. Every shudder. Every moan, every cry, *mine*. Every sound she ever made belonged to me, because I carved them into her. I made her remember the pitch, the rhythm, the surrender.

And now she gives that sound, my sound, to the witch? To the healer? To *them?*

How dare she.

They think Morgan is free. That she won't come when I call. That the leash I left under her ribs doesn't hum every time she breathes.

Idiots.

I will beckon.
And she will crawl.

The Elders once whispered that storm-bloods could not be leashed.
That they burned too wild, too bright. That the moment you tried to chain one, they'd turn to fire and consume you whole.

They were wrong.

I leashed the storm.
I *made her kneel.*
I carved obedience into her marrow and called it love.

And yet, she flinched.

It should not matter. It does not matter. She bends when I call. Her breath falters when I tug. Her pulse skips when I speak. But that flicker of rebellion, that trembling shred of will, it *gnaws*.

Because if Morgan ever remembers what she is, what she *was* before I took her, the throne I built on her obedience crumbles.

And they would burn me alive for daring to claim what the Council swore was untouchable.

So, I will crush her before she grows teeth again.

I didn't take her because I wanted her.
I took her because she was *useful*.
Because her pain made me powerful. Because when she knelt at my feet, the Council saw not weakness but proof.
They saw order. They saw control.

When I broke her, I built my crown.

And if the witch wants to chain herself to that ruin? Perfect. Two tethers are better than one. The witch will crawl just the same. She'll call it salvation, but every prayer she whispers will only tighten the leash.

When I call, she'll come.
They all will.

The mirror rippled.

I leaned closer, watching the scene inside twist like smoke in a jar. Morgan's head bowed. Joanna's hand brushed her temple. Lena's smirk cracked through the tension. The boys muttered in their corners.

For one heartbeat, they looked like a family.

Pathetic.

I pressed my palm flat against the glass, nails biting deep until my fingertips bled. Power flared through the room, the wards screaming in protest.

They think they've won her.
They think they've pulled her free.

But she's still mine.

She's *always* been mine.

I let the thought bloom into something sweet and venomous, then dragged my fingers down the glass. It rippled black. I reached through the bond, not enough to shatter her, just enough to remind her who owned the air she breathed.

Just enough to make her smile falter.

To make her breath catch.

To make her body remember.

The laughter on the other side of the mirror stuttered, fractured, then died altogether. The silence that followed was exquisite.

I smiled.

The glass glowed faint red, the sigil of my mark pulsing once before fading.

Still mine.
Always mine.
Even her silence belongs to me.

Chapter 38
The Cell
Morgan

The laughter died, but the tension stayed, thick as damp cloth, heavy as wet stone. It hung in the air between us, clinging to breath, impossible to shake off.

I didn't want to look at her. Not after everything.
Jo sat across from me, knees drawn to her chest, her head tilted down just enough to hide

her eyes. But I could still see the anger
trembling beneath her skin, see the way her
fingers dug into her arms like she was holding
herself together by force. Her eyes were
swollen, bloodshot, and her jaw was set so
tight I thought she might shatter her own teeth.

I sat with my knees pulled close, cuffs biting deep
into my wrists—cold metal pressed against the
pulse, each heartbeat a reminder that I was still
shackled. The skin there was rubbed raw. The
smell of iron hung thick—blood and rust, bleeding
together.

Lena crouched near me, her healer's kit
splayed open. Thread, salve, and bandages
caught the flickering torchlight, gleaming wet
in her hands. Her brow furrowed as she leaned
close to restitch what had torn open along my
side.

Zane and Ciaran muttered in the corner, their
voices low, words clipped sharp. Kael was quiet as
always—mask tilted toward the ground like he
was listening to something no one else could hear.

For a moment, just a breath, I almost believed the calm. That maybe this stillness was mercy. That maybe the storm had finally passed.

Then it started.

The slither.

It crept under my ribs first, faint as a twitch, subtle enough that I thought I'd imagined it. But then it deepened. A writhing pulse. A living coil tightening around my lungs.

I froze. The air turned heavy, too heavy. My chest ached.

"Please don't," I whispered. My voice was paper-thin. "Not now… not here…"

Joanna's eyes flicked up immediately, suspicion softening into concern. Lena's stitching stilled midair. The needle hung suspended, trembling between her fingers.

Then it hit,
The bond.

Like a serpent awakening, it coiled tight inside me, every muscle locking at once. The air vanished.

My spine arched. The breath tore out of my lungs, raw and ragged.
The cuffs clanged against the stone.

"Morgan?" Jo's voice cracked through the stillness. "What's happening?"

My ribs screamed. The pressure built, crushing down—harder, harder—until every breath felt like inhaling knives.

"Jo…" I rasped. "I…can't…"
The words fractured. My throat seized shut.

And then the bond yanked.

My body lurched forward so violently the chains snapped taut, jerking me back. The cuffs bit bone-deep. My body slammed into the wall, pain exploding white-hot through my ribs.

"Oh gods," I gasped. "What do I do? How…how do I get out of this?"

No answer.

The serpent squeezed tighter, its fangs sinking in. I could *feel* her, the ghost of Ines, whispering somewhere under my skin. *Come back. Come to me.*

I lunged again. Something tore.
A slick pop.
My shoulder slid clean out of its socket.

White pain flared behind my eyes. I screamed, silent, strangled, airless agony that shredded my throat.

Zane roared, shoving against his chains. "She's going to tear herself apart! See, Jo—she can't help it!"

Joanna

It didn't look real.

One second, Morgan had been breathing, barely, but steady. The next, she was gasping, convulsing, slamming against the chains like something unseen was puppeting her from inside.

I'd seen possession before, but never like this.

390

Her shoulder cracked with a sound I'll never forget. Her face contorted in pain, eyes wide and unseeing. Her body jerked against itself. She looked both alive and dead, her lungs a collapsing thing trying to claw for air.

Kael whispered something under his breath. Ciaran just stared, wide-eyed, horror and awe bleeding together.

And me? I froze. Because I didn't know how to save her.

Morgan

My lungs were collapsing. My vision flickered black.

"Jo! Lena!" I gasped between spasms. "Help me...please, I have to go, she's pulling me, I can't, breathe..."

Every word scraped raw out of me like glass dragged over bone.

"What do we do?" Jo screamed. "WHAT DO WE DO?"

"We don't know!" Lena cried, panic breaking her voice. "I can't heal what's inside her!"

The bond jerked again.
I choked. My hands clawed instinctively at the cuffs, tearing skin open.
The iron sliced through flesh, blood slicking my palms.

"Stop!" Jo shouted, voice splintering. "You're hurting yourself!"

"I can't!" I sobbed. "If I don't, it'll kill me!"

The first cuff cracked free with a wet, sucking sound. My wrist tore open, strips of skin peeling away, blood dripping in fat, heavy drops onto the stone.

I screamed through my teeth.

The bond yanked again, relentless. My body convulsed, dragged forward by invisible strings.

I threw all my weight against the second cuff. My ruined shoulder wrenched. Bone grated. Skin shredded down to the sinew. The world spun red and white and screaming.

Then —
It snapped.

Both hands free. Blood hot and slick between my fingers.

I dropped to my knees, chest heaving, chains dragging behind me like entrails.

For a moment, I thought that was it. That I was free.

But freedom didn't come.

The air still buzzed under my skin. The bond still whispered in my ear. The voice still breathed through my bones.

Come to me.

The pressure coiled once more, not in pain this time, but command.

My body moved before I could think. My feet dragged. My breath hitched.

I obeyed.

Because that's what the bond wanted. Because that's what I had been made to do.

CHAPTER 39
The Burn Behind
Joanna

Nothing could have prepared me for what unfolded in front of me.

Morgan slammed herself against the stone, over and over, until the sound became part of me. The scrape of metal, the choked breath between screams, the *crack* of her shoulder dislocating, those sounds are burned into me now. The sound wasn't human. It was wet and sharp, the way meat tears when you pull too hard.

Blood sprayed the floor in a mist that glittered under torchlight. I could *smell* it before I saw it, iron and salt, thick enough to taste.

And she kept going.
Ripping herself apart to get free.

Her skin tore in strips against the cuffs, the iron groaning before it finally gave way. When the metal hit the ground, it rang like a death bell, *clang*, heavy, final, echoing through the cavern until even the air trembled.

Then silence.
A terrible, suffocating silence.

And in that silence,
She moved.

Crawling. Dragging herself forward toward something none of us could see. Her body jerked in violent, broken movements, hands clawing at the ground, ribs heaving, every breath sounding like it might be her last.

It looked like she was chasing a ghost.
No, answering it.

Her lips moved soundlessly, but I knew that name.
I knew who was calling.

Ines.

That name burned behind my eyes.

And I realized, too late, that she'd been telling the truth all along. Every word.
The bond. The control. The way her body betrayed her.
Gods. I called her a liar. I accused her. I looked her in the eye and told her it was her fault.

And now she was bleeding out for it.

"I'm sorry," I whispered, but my throat was too raw for sound.

Morgan staggered to her feet. Her arms were ribbons of red, skin peeled and glistening in the dim light. Her breath came in ragged sobs, chest convulsing, eyes unfocused. She stumbled toward the door.

And no one stopped her.

The first to move was Ciaran.
He laughed.

The sound was jagged and awful, echoing in the stone cell like the crack of a whip. I snapped toward him, disbelief choking me.

"What the hell is wrong with you?" I shouted.

Zane's jaw clenched. He looked like he wanted to throw Ciaran through the wall.
Lena froze, her healer's kit trembling in her hands. Kael said nothing, his head tilted, as if listening to something distant and terrible that the rest of us couldn't hear.

Morgan was already gone.

Her blood painted the floor. Her cuffs lay open beside the drain. The echo of her sobs still trembled through the air.

And all I could think was *I did this.*

The tether inside me snapped hot, white-hot, like a brand pressed against my ribs. I doubled over, clutching my chest. It felt like the bond itself was punishing me for doubting her.

"MORGAN!" I screamed, the word shredding my throat. "I'm sorry! I'm so sorry I didn't believe you!"

The sound bounced back off stone walls, useless. She was too far gone.

> The smell of blood was everywhere now, metallic, suffocating, sharp. The torches sputtered against the damp, light flickering over the crimson smeared across the floor. My vision swam. I could feel her through the tether, faint but frantic, her fear, her pain, her desperation.

And then, nothing.

A blank pulse.
Silence.

> That silence broke something in me.

The cuffs bit down on my wrists like teeth. I looked at them—black steel gleaming, edges slick with my own blood from where I'd fought them before. My hands didn't feel like mine anymore. Just parts of the cage.

But I wasn't staying here.

I twisted my hands until the bone ached. Skin split. My thumb bent backward, tendons screaming. Pain shot up my arms in waves, but I didn't stop.

"Jo, stop…" Lena's voice cracked, trembling. "You're hurting yourself!"

"It's fine," I rasped, voice gone to sand. "I have to save her."

I yanked again. Fire ran down my arms, nerves burning alive. My breath came in broken sobs. The sound of tearing skin filled the air, sticky and wet.

Then, *pop.*
A cold rush.
Freedom.

I bit down hard on my lip to keep from screaming, the taste of copper bloomed across my tongue. Blood spilled down my wrists.

The other cuff was worse. The metal bit into the wound, cutting deeper with every pull. The smell of my own flesh burning from friction made me gag.

I didn't care.

I pulled until it gave.

Both cuffs hit the floor.

I stared down at my shaking hands, open, ruined, dripping. They trembled in the light, as if they didn't know what to do now that they were free.

Then I remembered.

I ran.

The cold stone scraped my bare feet. The air outside the cell was thick with torch smoke and damp earth, each breath cutting like frost. The tether burned brighter with every step, pulling, dragging, *leading.*

"Morgan," I whispered. "I'm coming."

I ran through the corridor, past the bloodstained stones, past Lena's voice shouting behind me. Every heartbeat echoed like a war drum.

The tunnel narrowed, wind howling through cracks in the rock. Somewhere in the distance, thunder rolled, deep, guttural, hungry.

And I kept running.

Because I loved her. Gods help me, I loved that woman. Even when she ruined me. Even when she burned everything she touched.

I would follow her into the fire.

I would bleed before letting her die again.

CHAPTER 40
The Room with no doors
Morgan

The cuffs struck the stone with a heavy *clang* that rang through the corridor like a bell tolling for my body.
Before I even had time to breathe, the bond yanked me forward.

It wasn't a pull, it was a *possession*.
Claws raked beneath my ribs, dragging me from the inside out, peeling me raw. Each step scraped fire through my bones, every tendon screaming for mercy. My wrists were blood to the bone, my shoulder swollen and hot, the

stitches in my stomach stretched until they felt ready to burst.

None of it mattered. It never did.
The bond called. And I obeyed.

But underneath that pull, faint, stubborn, unyielding, something else pulsed.
The tether.
Joanna.

It ached like a second heartbeat, one pulling me forward, the other dragging me back. The two forces collided until my chest was a battlefield — bond against tether, obedience against love. My body convulsed between them, torn open by what it wanted and what it was forced to do.

I couldn't scream. My throat was too tight. The only sound left was the pulse in my skull.

Joanna's voice followed behind me — faint, broken, begging.
"I'm sorry," she cried. "Morgan, I'm so sorry."

The words hit me harder than the chains ever had.
Then the corridor swallowed me whole.

The air was damp and metallic. Every breath stuck to my tongue like rust. The walls closed in around the sound of my own heartbeat, boom, boom, *boom, boom,* until it drowned out thought itself.

Then the door appeared.

It wasn't there before, it never was. But the bond carved a path through the dark until it stood in front of me, wide open, waiting like a velvet mouth ready to devour.

The room beyond dripped red.

Satin drapes bled from ceiling to floor. Silver light shimmered across a platform carved from black stone. Incense burned thick and sweet, masking the stench of iron and old blood. Heat rolled off the walls like breath.

It would have been beautiful if it wasn't hell.

And she was there.

Ines stood in the center, calm, perfect, predatory. Her smile was a blade wrapped in silk.

"Morgan," she purred, voice low and venom-smooth. "There you are, my little pet."
Her eyes slid down my torn wrists, the blood, the trembling. "Now you'll learn what happens when you disobey me."

The platform glowed under lamplight, red satin stretched over stone, silver etchings spiraling in runes I couldn't read. Four posts rose from the corners like spears, the canopy above them black as void.

It was a stage. It always was.

"Kneel," she said. "Undress. Do as I say."

My muscles betrayed me first. My knees buckled. My hands trembled to unfasten the ruined fabric on my shoulders. Sweat slicked my skin. Blood pooled warm between my fingers. I wanted to fight, to run, to throw myself into the wall until something gave. But my body didn't belong to me anymore.

I kneeled.

Her heels clicked behind me; *tap, tap, tap,* slow and certain, a rhythm of ownership.

"You dare look at another woman," she murmured, breath brushing my ear. "You will be corrected for that."

Her hand traced my spine, lingering over the scar burned into my flesh.
The brand flared alive, heat searing through muscle, lighting my nerves like fuse wire.

"You're trembling," she whispered. "You used to beg for this."

Then the first strike.

A crack of magic split the air. Pain bloomed bright, sharp, blinding, intimate. Another strike followed. Then another. Each one harder, deeper, the rhythm cruelly precise. My breath broke on every hit until it turned raw, choked, unrecognizable.

She kissed each welt she made, lips soft, words sweeter than rot. "See?" she cooed. "Your body remembers me."

My vision blurred. I couldn't tell where pain ended and shame began.

Ines circled me, her perfume thick enough to choke. "You know the best game, little storm?" she said, almost playful. "Your witch will come. I'll tie her up, and you'll help me break her. I'll make you watch me bond her piece by piece."

My stomach turned to acid.
No. Not Jo. Not her.

The tether flared so bright it seared through my ribs. I could *feel* her now, close. Too close.

And then I heard it.
A breath.
A gasp.

I turned my head, just enough to see her shadow in the doorway.

"Jo..." My voice shattered. "You have to run! It's a trap!"

For one miraculous heartbeat, the bond faltered.
Then it retaliated.

Pain tore through me like a blade twisting through my lungs. I doubled over, screaming. The sound was ripped from my throat, stolen midair.

Ines only smiled. "Ah," she sighed. "There she is."

The door slammed and shut behind Joanna. The ward seals shimmered black, sealing us in.

Joanna's voice cut through the air, fierce and trembling. "You can do anything to me, but don't touch her again."

It should've broken me. It did.

She climbed onto the platform. The air thickened, heat closing around us until every breath hurt.

Ines purred. "Sweet witch. Always so noble. So predictable. You'll make a beautiful example."

"No, Jo," I whispered. "You shouldn't have come. Seeing you here—will ruin me."

Iron cuffs lifted from the platform, serpents of metal that coiled around Joanna's wrists. They yanked her back, snapping shut with the sound of bone meeting steel. Her gasp sliced the air.

Ines reached for a dagger.

> Not just any dagger, the dagger.
> Curved. Silver. Still stained with my blood.

My body convulsed at the sight. The memory hit before the thought: the ritual, the blade, the pain, her hand pressing it into me while she whispered I was hers.

> "You know the best part?" Ines said softly, admiring the blade as if it were art. "My favorite punishment hasn't even begun."

She pointed it at Joanna. "She'll kneel," she said. Then she turned it on me. "While I ruin you and keep you as mine."

> Joanna's magic flared bright — salt-white veins of light crawling up her arms. "You're sick," she spat. "She's not yours."

Ines laughed, unbothered. "She begged for me once," she crooned. "Did you hear her tonight? The way she sounded. She *wanted* me."

"No," I choked out. "Don't—please don't."

"See?" Ines smiled. "She still begs."

Joanna's jaw tightened. "You never owned her. And you won't own me." Her mark burned brighter, lighting her from the inside out.

Ines's eyes gleamed. "That's what I love most, when they fight."

The tether ignited. The bond constricted.
Pain exploded through me, every nerve aflame, every vein a current of fire.

I met Joanna's eyes.

Horror. Love. Fury.
All of it there, tangled together.

And I knew.

She was trapped.
I was breaking.
And Ines was winning.

The room had no doors.
There was nowhere left to run.

CHAPTER 41

The Severing

Joanna

I was lying there for what felt like an eternity.

The dagger pressed hard against my ribs, cold at first, then unbearably hot as it dragged down. It wasn't a slice; it was a *statement*. Each pull deliberate, each burn a declaration of control.

The cut was shallow, not enough to kill, but enough to sting, enough to make my chest rise and fall with each ragged breath. The air felt sharp, tasting of iron. I clenched my jaw, swallowing the scream clawing its way up my throat. I would not give Ines the satisfaction.

411

The tether pulsed under my skin. It screamed her name, Morgan.

She looked so small across the platform. Shaking. Pale. Trembling like she could will the pain out of me if she just stared hard enough. Then she looked away, as if seeing it might break her open.

Ines pressed harder, her smile delicate and vicious. The dagger trailed lower, scraping across my abdomen until blood welled hot and slow. The air filled with its scent, metal and salt. My breath hitched, then tore into a sound that barely resembled me.

"INES!" I gasped. "You don't have to do this!"

My cry cracked through the chamber. Blood ran thick down my side, sticky against my clothes.

Morgan's nails splintered against the stone, her hands scraping until they bled. A hiss broke from her throat, sharp, broken, a sound that didn't belong to her but to something deeper. Pain was traveling through her like it belonged to both of us.

Ines's eyes glittered like polished glass. She turned the blade toward my witchmark, tracing the glow beneath my skin.

"You wear this like a crown," she murmured, voice dripping with fascination. "Let's see what you are without it."

The witchmark burned. The light beneath my skin thrashed like a trapped thing. My pulse roared in my ears. My muscles trembled as the blade hovered, its edge glinting pale blue.

Across the platform, Morgan lifted her head. Our eyes locked. Just for a second. Terrified. Pleading.

Then she looked away again—because she couldn't bear it.

Ines's dagger grazed my mark. Pain tore white-hot through me,
And then,

"NO!"

Morgan's scream ripped through the air like thunder. It wasn't a sound, it was a war cry. The kind that shakes gods.

Ines flinched, snapping her head toward her. "You dare defy me?"

A metallic *CLANG*.

Lena's blade flashed silver as she cut through my restraints. The chains clattered to the floor like dead snakes.

Ines turned on her, fury twisting her face. "How dare you…"

She didn't finish. Morgan was already moving.

She slammed into Ines with a sound that wasn't human, bone against stone, breath against fury. I heard the wet *crick-crick-crick* of ribs and shoulder and bone protesting.

"MORGAN! STOP! YOU'LL DIE!" My scream tore through me as I lunged forward, grabbing her, dragging her back before she could break herself in half.

Lena's magic flared, a white burst that cracked through the chamber like lightning. The force threw Ines backward, her body slamming into the far wall with a violent *CRACK!*

Dust rained from the ceiling. The air trembled.

I caught Morgan as she collapsed, her breath ragged, her body shaking. Blood slicked her chin. "Morgan, no, no, please," I whispered. "Stay with me."

Her chest heaved. Her pulse fluttered weak beneath my hand.

"Oh gods, Morgan."

And then—

Morgan

The moment I struck Ines, everything inside me shattered.

The tether yanked me toward Joanna. The bond dragged me toward Ines. The two forces collided, ripping through my body with all the

415

violence of storm and stone. My lungs split open.
My veins screamed. I couldn't breathe, couldn't
see, couldn't tell which pain belonged to me.

But when I saw that dagger pressed to Joanna's
witchmark,
I didn't care.

I moved anyway.

> I hit Ines like a storm breaking through glass.
> The impact lit my vision with white spots. My
> ribs cracked, my shoulder shrieked, my throat
> caught fire, but my hands closed over her
> wrists, and I wrenched the dagger away before
> she could bury it in Joanna's skin.

Then Jo's hands were on me, dragging, pulling,
wrapping around my shaking frame. I didn't
know if she was holding me together or keeping
me from falling apart.

> Lena's magic flared again, bright as salt fire.
> Ines flew back, crashing into the wall with a
> sound that made the whole room shudder.

Jo turned me to face her. Her hands were shaking, but steady. Her eyes, gods, her eyes, were all fire and sorrow and something I didn't deserve.

"I'm so sorry, Jo…" I managed, the words cracked and broken.

"No," she said fiercely. "I'm sorry. I should have believed you."

She pressed her forehead to mine. Her palm cupped the back of my neck. The warmth of her touch sank deep, and her salt-light magic spread through me, burning, soothing, alive.

It crawled down my spine, seeping into bone. For a moment, I thought it was healing. For a moment, I thought I could breathe.

Then her hand brushed the brand.

Agony tore through me. My body arched back, a strangled scream ripping out of me. My vision whited out.

"Jo! Please!" I gasped.

"Tell me to stop," she whispered. "Say it, and I will."

417

I didn't.

Because even through the pain, something was changing. Her light was sinking into me— fighting something black and twisted and wrong. The brand burned so hot I could feel the mark blister, then crack, then split.

Joanna

All I wanted was to hold her. To keep her breathing. To make her whole again.

My magic surged wild beneath my skin. Salt-light burned through every vein. I pressed my hand flat between her shoulder blades, right over the scar. My light poured into her, crawling through the broken channels like liquid fire.

She convulsed beneath my touch, her back arching, every muscle trembling. The brand blazed bright purple beneath my palm.

I didn't let go.

I couldn't.

Dark tendrils coiled up my wrist, thick, alive, writhing. The bond. Its color was wrong, deep violet, almost black, pulsing like a heartbeat.

I wrapped my light tighter around it. Salt met smoke. Violet clashed with white.

And then—*crack.*

The sound was sharp and final, like glass shattering under a scream.

My breath caught. "Morgan…" I whispered. "I think your bond, it's breaking."

Her eyes flew open, glowing faint. "Joanna!"

"I'm here," I said, steady, even as my tears fell hot against her skin.

"It hurts," she choked. "It hurts so much."

"I know," I whispered. "I've got you. Breathe with me. Just breathe."

Our foreheads pressed together. Our breaths tangled, hers shaky, mine steady. For one second, I thought she might die in my arms. For one second, I thought we might both burn.

And then—

The doors burst open.

Light flooded in, harsh, holy, cruel.

> The Elders stormed through, robes flaring like wings. Their staffs glowed blue-white, voices raised in a chorus that felt like knives.

"ENOUGH!" one thundered, the word shaking the chamber.

> Behind them, Zane, Ciaran, Kael; charging in like men who'd already lost everything and refused to lose one more thing.

Morgan

The violet light inside me shattered.

> The bond cracked down the center, splitting into shards of smoke and fire. Each break sent sparks scattering across my skin, burning out before they could scar.

It tore free of my ribs. My lungs. My spine. Every hook that had ever been buried in me ripped loose, leaving behind only light and ruin.

The pain was holy. Terrifying. Cleansing.

Then—silence.

The chamber went still. The torches went out. The air hummed like the pause before it rains.

And for the first time in years
I couldn't feel her.

The bond was gone.

I fell into Joanna's arms, trembling, shaking, half-alive. The air around us still smelled of ozone and salt and blood.

She held me close, her tears falling against my neck.

I couldn't speak, but I didn't need to. She knew. She always did.

Joanna

I pressed my lips to her forehead, sobbing.
"Morgan," I whispered, "you're free."

Behind us, chaos roared. The Elders shouted, the
boys fought, the world burned.

But none of it mattered.

The chamber reeked of ruin, ash, salt, metal.
Smoke curled from the broken marks in the floor.

And Morgan, my beautiful, stubborn, broken
Morgan, sobbed against my chest.

Not from pain.
From release.

And I cried with her.

Because the bond was gone.
Because she was free.
Because, for the first time since the world began,
she was mine, and she was *herself*.

CHAPTER 42
Enemies of the Court
Joanna

The silence was deafening.

Smoke curled in the air, soft and gray, ghosting through the ruin of the chamber. Morgan sobbed into my shoulder, her body shaking but finally at ease. Her breath came out in short, broken gasps against my neck. Her skin was hot and slick with blood, her pulse trembling under my fingertips like something alive and fragile.

For the first time since I met her, she looked unbound.

"You don't have to be scared anymore," I whispered into her hair, voice trembling against the chaos. "I've got you."

The Elders stirred through the dust like ghosts made of rage. Their robes dragged across the stone, heavy with soot and blood. The air warped around them, thick with incense, ozone, and the sharp bite of spent magic.

"YOU WILL CEASE THIS BLASPHEMY!"

Erelith's voice cracked through the wreckage, a sound like thunder inside bone. The floor shuddered beneath us, stones splitting.

Another Elder; jeweled, gilded, gleaming through smoke, lifted a trembling hand toward the ceiling. His voice was a hiss. "You've unmade our sanctioned rite." His eyes were knives. "You've unmade the order itself."

"No," I said, my voice steady, but breaking at the edges. "I unmade your prison."

My gaze snapped toward them, fire crawling beneath my skin. "You curse me like I'm the sinner, when you're the ones who stole her rights away."

From the haze behind me came movement—steady, deliberate.

Zane, Kael, and Ciaran stepped over the bodies that lined the floor. Their blades dripped red. Their faces were carved from fury and defiance. They took position in a half-circle around us, shoulders squared, breath heaving like a pack of wolves that had finally decided to bite back.

Zane's voice broke first—loud, rough, raw. "You call this sanctioned?" he shouted. "You call this holy? It's not, it's cruelty!"

Ciaran laughed, sharp and wild, like a spark catching dry grass.
"Finally," he said, breathless. "I thought we'd rot under this Court forever but look at us. We're finally tearing it apart."

Kael said nothing. His silence was a storm lightning flickering across his hands, his eyes locked on the Elders like a blade about to fall.

Around us, the factions stirred.

> The Gilded raised their hammers, jewels
> pulsing like dying suns.
> The Hollow whispered from the corners, voices
> like oil sliding across stone.
> The Dreadmarked laughed, their teeth catching
> the light.
> The Antlered bristled, antlers rattling, eyes
> glowing beneath the torches.

Then one stepped forward. His antlers glinted
with gold dust, his expression carved in rage.

> "Brother," Thalos said, his voice low and
> venomous. "What the hell are you doing?"

Zane's jaw tightened. His sword gleamed under
the firelight.
"I'm standing on the right side today."

> Thalos's sneer split like a wound. "You're
> standing on the losing one."

The floor began to shake. Dust rained from the
ceiling. The air itself felt alive, humming with
magic and hatred.

Erelith raised his hand, fingers dripping with energy bright as molten gold. His eyes locked on me.

He didn't hesitate.

The spell tore from his palm with a sound like screaming metal.

The world burned white.

And then—Lena.

She burst from the shadows, a flash of motion and defiance. Her blade caught the light midair, cutting through the spell with a flare that split the chamber apart. Sparks cascaded down like rain. The steel sang.

"It was never your decision," she said. Her voice rang through the hall clear, strong, final. "And now you'll be the ones who suffer."

Her sword struck the stone.

And the world split open.

Light poured upward, golden and furious. It ripped through the floor, through the air, through time itself. The walls bowed outward. The torches blew out. The chamber screamed.

The Rift yawned wide, alive, violent, hungry.

Stone cracked. Air tore. The scent of iron and ash filled every breath.

The Elders staggered, their chants breaking on their tongues. Their power fizzled into smoke. Ines stumbled through the chaos, bloodied but smiling grin too wide, too calm. The Rift's light carved her features into something almost divine, almost monstrous.

Lena's body glowed. The sword trembled in her hands. She didn't flinch.
She vanished first.
Swallowed whole by the light she had called.

"Morgan!" I screamed.

Her hand slipped from mine, wet with blood.

"MORGAN!"

I lunged for her, caught her fingertips for one heartbeat, and then the ground gave way.

The Rift swallowed us both.

"JO, MORGAN! NO!"

Zane's voice tore through the roar. He jumped after us, blade and body flashing as the light devoured him.

"Fuck!" Ciaran bellowed. "They've really got me dying for them again!" He dove next, laughter and terror mingled in his throat.

Kael sprinted forward, lightning crackling over his arms, but the floor caved. The scream that left him was swallowed by the Rift as he fell.

Thalos stayed behind. His face was the last thing I saw, a portrait of fury and loss as the Rift sealed like a wound, dividing blood from blood.

The tether yanked me forward.

My body spun through a maelstrom of heat and shadow.
Morgan tumbled below me, her hair a streak of fire in the light.

The air burned. The magic howled. Gravity dissolved.

We were falling. We were burning.
We were unmaking everything.

    The last thing I saw before the world came
    undone was the factions turning on the Court,
    the Gilded clashing with the Antlered,
    the Dreadmarked laughing as they carved
    through their own,
    the Hollow melting into shadow,
    and the Elders screaming as the Rift devoured
    them whole.

And then—

Nothing

CHAPTER 43
Court Debate
Erelith

The chamber still reeked of salt and smoke. It clung to the throat, metallic, bitter, the sour tang of a wound that won't close. The Rift had torn the stone open like an old scar; light bled from the fissure in thin, angry veins that pulsed with a heat that made the soles of my boots sweat. I leaned on my staff because upright felt like an accusation; because if I didn't, my legs would give under the weight of what had happened. Not that they would ever see me falter.

"She undid it," I said. My voice rasped. The words sounded smaller than they should. "The witch severed the bond, and now the Rift grows wider with every hour."

The Elders circled me like vultures arranged themselves around carrion. Their robes smoked at the hems; their faces were pale, tight, fear masquerading as composure. None of them spoke first. To name it aloud would be to admit that our law could be unmade.

"They'll call it freedom," one of the Gilded said, voice slick as oil. He tapped his jeweled hammer; it pulsed faintly with light as if to reassure him. "But it's rot. Blasphemy. If word spreads that bonds can be broken, everything we built collapses."

I tightened my grip on the staff until the wood complained. The stone underfoot hummed. "Then we remind them. We show them what happens to those who defy us."

The Hollowed

Shadows slid along the walls like smoke finding cracks. Their whispers were thin and wet, voices that never quite landed on a name.

"They tremble," one breathed.

"They falter," another answered, the sound slipping like oil between stones.

"Erelith rattles like a leaf in the wind," a voice said with a hiss that tasted of old cellars and colder things.

> Laughter rose, not loud, but present, folding into the chamber like mildew. It crept between the Elders' words, a cold thing that made the hairs on the back of the neck stand up.

"They pretend to be strong," the Hollowed said. "This proves they can break." The laughter curled tighter, promising.

"Perhaps," another whispered, "it is time we decide whether the Elders are still worth following."

The Dreadmarked

I leaned my back to a shattered pillar, the red glow from the fissure painting the cracks like veins. The Elders argued; the room smelled of old incense and new panic. Beautiful, all of it — so very beautiful.

"Let them preach," I said, low and satisfied. "Let them clutch their laws like prayer beads. It won't save them."

Laughter rolled through my throat, mean and easy. "War fattens the weak," I said. "Chaos is a feast. When the witch and the fae return, we'll pluck what the Court fears to touch. Their downfall will be our boon."

The other Dreadmarked grinned in the torchlight, teeth catching fire like little knives. Appetite sharpened.

Thalos (The Antlered)

I stood in the back, half in shadow, arms folded. The fissure's light crawled over my boots; it looked almost alive, like the country's veins had ruptured. People say I look like Zane. Maybe. He wears fire. I carry calculus and quiet.

434

"My brother chose the wrong side," I told the warrior beside me, voice low and brittle. "But maybe he isn't wrong about rot."

The fissure cracked again beneath our feet, a soft grinding that felt like a throat clearing. I studied it not with fear but with math: what falls will let you climb, who is left to climb with you, and what you can rip from the ashes afterwards.

"If the Rift swallows them both," I said, "the Court dies. And from that ruin, who decides what rises?" The question hung between us like a blade.

Silence answered.

Ines

I hovered at the edge, where torchlight bled into black. I let them claw. Let them rend one another apart on the stage. They were predictable: frightened mice gnawing at old laws.

"Threads unravel," I murmured, tracing a pale finger down the heated wall where the Rift's shimmer still quivered. The skin where my nails passed cooled and the stone remembered pressure.

A small smile picked at the corner of my mouth. Let them think they won. Let them clutch at vengeance and law. When the world splits again, and it will split; I will stand at the seam, needle between my teeth, ready to stitch what I want into the tear.

Erelith

Enough. Their voices clattered; they grated like metal on stone until I slammed the staff down and the sound cut them like a blade. The room held its breath.

"The Rift is not closed," I said. "The tether is not ended. This is not the end. If anything, this is the beginning of war."

They looked at me then. Eyes like mines. Some with heat, some with temper. In their faces you could already see the map of alliances change.

Below us, the fissure spoke again — a deep, rolling crack that crawled up through the soles of our boots and into the ribs. It was a promise, or a threat. The stone shifted, a slow, insistent pulse.

No one argued. The silence that followed was heavy as bone. The Rift breathed. The Court listened. And somewhere in the dark between the wards, the world tilted.

Chapter 44

The Rift
Morgan

It did not feel like flying.

It felt like I was falling for hours with no end, no bottom, no gravity, just a plummet through a throat of fire. Pain seared through me like paper ripping, ribs splintering, cracking hot white, breaking and resetting again and again. My joints snapped like wet twigs. Dizziness swallowed me whole until I wasn't sure if I still had a body at all.

438

Something dragged a hollow scrape down my spine, like a boned finger pressing into each vertebrae, something old and hungry unthreading me as if I had never existed. Every atom shrieked apart and then stitched back wrong. I screamed until time lost shape, until I was certain I had been falling for years. Rebreaking. Recalibrating.

A clock tolled inside my skull — DING. DING. DING. — centuries of hurt striking like bells. Each toll shook my teeth, my tongue, my thoughts. The air tasted of salt though there was none, only smoke, thick and warm, erasing me more with every breath. It filled my collapsing lungs, coated them like oil. It smelled like temples, gasoline, and pyres set ablaze. Bells rang louder than my heartbeat. Louder than thought. I bit my lips until I tasted iron, desperate for anything but the phantom taste of salt.

Then softness brushed my cheek. Hair, Joanna's hair, weightless beside me in the void.

A shape stirred in the dark. It was not flesh but pressure. A presence, golden fingertips patient and old, gravity itself forcing me upward. It touched the hollow where the tether had lived, kindling a single spark.

Joanna's voice threaded through the cracks of time.

"Morgan."

The name did not come from outside me. It rose from somewhere buried so deep I wondered if it had always been my name — or another language borrowing my skin. It was not Joanna's voice exactly, but something that slid under mine and warmed the broken places, coaxing them toward healing.

Then the world ripped open.

I hit the ground with a breath that tore my chest raw. The impact knocked me animal-raw, smoke clawing at my throat, something sweet and metallic on my tongue. My knees skidded against cold stone; my palms blistered where they scraped. My heart thumped like a thing trying to claw out.

And then, I was whole.

No shattered ribs. No brand crawling across my skin. Whole in the impossible way that makes your body feel borrowed.

I rolled onto my back. The ceiling was not the one I remembered. The plaster cracked differently. Candlelight flickered the way it always had in a room I once loved, familiar as a lullaby, wrong in the margins.

Caerthwyn. The word rose like a hymn.
Home.

The bed was made. A gown hung neatly.
The garden beyond the window smelled
of cloves and wet earth, not ash.

Too clean. Too soon.

I stumbled to the mirror. My face blinked
back at me, skin unbruised, eyes bright,
younger by years. My hands flew to my
back, my collarbone. Blank. No scars.

"Oh gods."

The words were half relief, half terror.

Memory unraveled in threads. I knew
enough. I knew what was coming. Ines
had not touched me yet. Not looked at
me like glass. Not carved ownership into
my skin. Not yet.

442

But the ache was already there. A bruise forming around a hollow with a name I could not say, who I missed I don't know.

> I could not place her face. I could not place the sound of her laugh. But the space she had filled in me still ached, raw and hot, as if someone had seared me and left only the outline of her hand across my back.

Her memory began to unravel.

I did not know her name. But I was already undone. A ghost of safety. A promise. A hunger that tasted like grief.

Joanna

It tasted like salt.

Not sea-salt. Not the sprinkle-over-your-shoulder kind. This was the salt of knives and promises, metallic, sharp, the sting you feel before a tear falls. It sat on my tongue and refused to leave, scratching the roof of my mouth like a thing that remembered being owed.

First the light went.
Then the sound.
Then me.

The fall was not fast. It was slow and petty, like drowning through syrup. Time stretched until every second could be accused of cruelty.

Then grass.

My knees hit hard; the earth was wet and soft in a way that made my fingers ache. My breath came in shaky puffs. Salt still coated my teeth.

Morning light bled through the trees. They were pale and tidy, the kind that makes you pretend everything is fine. The forest smelled of damp wood and something like cloves. Halewyck — and not the burned version I knew. Not hostile. Not watching. Just ordinary, which made it dangerous.

I knew the place before my mind caught up. Not merely remembering the path. I knew it like a bone remembering where it belongs.

Then a voice.

Not hers.

I walked toward it.

Because it was home.

Mama was alive again.

Epilogue
Antlered Unease
Zane

The fall stole my breath
but not my fire.

> One heartbeat I was in the chamber, blades
> slick, shouting Joanna's name.
> The next, I was ripped through light and heat,
> through a wound in the world itself.
> The Rift swallowed me whole.

I don't remember landing. Only the *fall*.
The drop that never ended.
The smoke that filled my lungs.
The phantom ache of antlers splitting through my
skull even though none were there.

> I remember reaching for them, Joanna, Morgan,
> and catching only air.

When I opened my eyes, I was standing in the
middle of a battle ring. The sand was dark with
old blood. The crowd roared above me, faceless,
blurred in shadow. My sword was already in my
hand, though I didn't remember drawing it.
Across from me stood a man I didn't know. His
armor shimmered faintly gold. His eyes, wrong.
Too bright. Too sure.

The air smelled of iron and rain. The wind was
sharp with pine. **Antlered lands.** My home.
But not the same. The trees leaned too close, their
branches heavy with rot. The sky pulsed faintly
red at the edges, as if the world itself were still
bleeding from the Rift.

> I pressed a hand to my chest. The tether burned
> there, faint and foreign. It wasn't mine, but I
> could feel the echo of it—a bond broken, a
> scream swallowed. It wasn't my pain, but I
> carried it anyway.

The others weren't here. No Joanna. No Morgan.
No Ciaran. No Kael. Just me and the quiet between
battle cries.

And in that quiet, something moved.

A whisper slid through the wind, low and ancient:

"War is coming."

It wasn't a voice. Not truly. It was a memory sinking into bone, *old Antlered dread.* The kind that doesn't speak in words, only in warnings.

I gripped my blade tighter and looked up at the trees that had once sheltered me.
For the first time, I wondered if they would stand with me or against me when the war began.

Because the Rift hadn't just stolen us.
It had *split* us.
It had changed everything.

And somewhere beyond the horizon, my brother Thalos was still watching from the other side, waiting for the moment I would have to choose whether to fight beside him or against him.

Epilogue
First Sight
Lena

The Rift spat me out like a stone from a sling.

One heartbeat I was in the Court—sword blazing, splitting stone.
The next, I was choking on smoke, dragged through a wound in the world.

Then came *grass*.

I hit hard enough to rattle every bone in my body. The air was cold and wet, heavy with the smell of rain and earth. My fingers locked around the hilt of my sword. It still hummed with faint light, pulsing in rhythm with my heartbeat—as if the Rift itself hadn't let go of me yet.

When I lifted my head, I saw her.

449

She stood a few yards away, unsteady but upright, as if she'd crawled through the same fire. Her skin shimmered with a pale blue almost translucent, light rippling across it like reflections on water. Wings unfurled behind her: vast, silent, and strange. Not feathered. Not flesh. Something in between, glowing faintly where dawn kissed them.

She wasn't human. Not even close.

Her eyes lifted to mine, wide and searching. Ocean eyes, flecked with green, bright enough to hold the horizon itself. My breath caught.

The ground between us hummed, low and deep, as if the Rift hadn't truly closed but was waiting, listening, for what would happen next.

She took a step toward me.
I raised my sword.

The air trembled.
The light shifted.

And somewhere beyond the trees, something answered.

Epilogue

Reaching but never touching
Joanna

The dream felt too real to be a dream.

The ground was soft and cold beneath my feet, mist curling around my ankles like breath. The air smelled faintly of rain and smoke. My heartbeat sounded too loud in the quiet.

There was a pull under my skin—steady, familiar, like someone calling my name from far away.

"Morgan?"

The name slipped out before I could stop it. It felt *old* in my mouth, like I'd said it a hundred times before.

Through the fog, a shape appeared.

A woman stood ahead, framed in pale light.
Her hair shimmered like ink and her wings
glowed faintly—gold brushed with shadow.
My chest ached.

"Is it you?" I whispered.

She didn't answer. But she looked up, and her eyes
caught mine. The fog thinned between us.

Morgan

I've had this dream before,
but never this clear.

> The world was quiet, still, full of light that
> didn't belong to any sun. I could smell salt and
> smoke. My body felt heavy, but my heart
> raced.

And then I saw her.

> A figure in the haze.
> Hair like sunlight.
> Eyes I couldn't name but knew I'd loved.

"Joanna."

452

The name burned on my tongue. I reached out without thinking. My hand trembled. The air between us rippled.

Joanna

She moved first. Then I did.
I reached back, fingers stretching through the mist.

I could almost feel her,
the warmth, the pulse of something real.

The air hummed, bright and alive.
The space between us shrank until one more step could have closed it.

Morgan

Our hands almost touched.

The warmth was right there, bleeding through the air.
It was everything I didn't know I was missing.

Joanna

The world shook.

Light fractured between us like a mirror
breaking. The mist rushed in, swallowing her
whole.

Morgan

I tried to hold on, but the dream slipped
through my fingers.
Her face faded first.
Then the warmth.
Then everything.

Joanna

I woke with my hand still outstretched, my palm
warm, my chest aching,
like I'd lost something I couldn't name.

Morgan

When I opened my eyes, the world was new
and wrong.
But I could still feel her.
Somewhere.

Both

Reaching—
but never touching.